Indian Certificate of Secondary Education Examination

Model Specimen Papers

COMPUTER APPLICATIONS

General Instructions for Students

(Two hours)

Answers to this Paper must be written on the paper provided separately.
*You will **not** be allowed to write during the first **15 minutes**.*
This time is to be spent in reading the question paper.
The time given at the head of this Paper is the time allowed for writing the answers.
This paper is divided into two Sections.
*Attempt **all** questions from **Section A** and **any four** questions from **Section B**.*
The intended marks for questions or parts of questions are given in brackets [ ].

(All Rights Reserved)

OSWAL PUBLISHERS

Head office : 1/12, Sahitya Kunj, M.G. Road, Agra-282 002
Phone : (0562) 2527771– 4
E-mail : contact@oswalpublishers.com, sales@oswalpublishers.com
Website : www.oswalpublishers.com
Facebook link : https://www.facebook.com/oswalpublishersindia
Also available on : amazon.in, Flipkart, snapdeal

CONTENTS

Model Specimen Paper 1 3–10

Model Specimen Paper 2 11–16

Model Specimen Paper 3 (Unsolved) 17–18

Model Specimen Paper 4 19–24

Model Specimen Paper 5 25–30

Model Specimen Paper 6 (Unsolved) 31–32

Model Specimen Paper 7 33–37

Model Specimen Paper 8 38–42

Model Specimen Paper 9 (Unsolved) 43–44

Model Specimen Paper 10 45–50

Model Specimen Paper 11 51–56

Model Specimen Paper 12 (Unsolved) 57-58

Model Specimen Paper 13 59–64

Model Specimen Paper 14 65–69

Model Specimen Paper 15 (Unsolved) 70–71

Model Specimen Paper 16 72–76

Model Specimen Paper 17 77–83

Model Specimen Paper 18 (Unsolved) 84–85

Model Specimen Paper 19 86–90

Model Specimen Paper 20 91–94

Model Specimen Paper 21 (Unsolved) 95–96

Edition : 2018

ISBN : 978-93-87660-34-2

ICSE Model Specimen Papers are available in the following subjects :

HINDI	HISTORY & CIVICS	ECONOMIC APPLICATIONS
ENGLISH-I	MATHEMATICS	COMPUTER APPLICATIONS
ENGLISH-II	PHYSICS	COMMERCIAL APPLICATIONS
GEOGRAPHY	BIOLOGY	ECONOMICS
COMPLETE COURSE (WORKBOOK) IN ENGLISH-I : X		**COMPLETE COURSE IN ENGLISH-II : XI & XII**
COMPLETE COURSE (WORKBOOK) IN ENGLISH-I : XII		**COMPLETE COURSE IN HINDI : XI & XII**

MODEL SPECIMEN PAPER–1

SECTION—A

SECTION A (40 Marks)
*Attempt **all** questions.*

Question 1.

(a) Define abstraction. [2]

(b) Differentiate between searching and sorting. [2]

(c) Write a difference between the functions isUpperCase( ) and toUpperCase( ). [2]

(d) How are private members of a class different from public members ? [2]

(e) Classify the following as primitive or non-primitive datatypes : [2]

    (i) char   (ii) arrays   (iii) int

    (iv) classes

Answer :

(a) It is the act of representing essential features without including the background details.

(b)

Searching	Sorting
It is the process of checking whether the element is present in the array or not.	It is the process of arranging the data in the array.
Types of searching techniques are linear and binary search.	Types of sorting techniques are exchange selection and bubble sort.

(c)

isUpperCase()	toUpperCase()
This function is used to check whether a character is in upper case or not.	This function is used to convert a character in upper case.
Return type is boolean.	Return type is char.

(d)

Private Members	Public Members
It is the most restricted access specifier.	It is the least restricted access specifier.
Members declared under this section are only accessible in their own class.	Members declared under this section are accessible in all parts of a java program.

(e) primitive : (i) char, (iii) int

    non-primitive : (ii) arrays, (iv) classes

Question 2.

(a) (i) int res = 'A'; [2]

       What is the value of res ? [2]

    (ii) Name the package that contains wrapper classes.

(b) State the difference between while and do while loop. [2]

(c) System.out.print ("BEST");

    System.out.println ("OF LUCK");

    Choose the correct option for the output of the above statements

    (i) BEST OF LUCK

    (ii) BEST

        OF LUCK

(d) Write the prototype of a function check which takes an integer as an argument and returns a character. [2]

(e) Write the return data type of the following function. [2]

    (i) endsWith( )

    (ii) log( )

Answer 2.

(a) (i) res=65 (ii) java.lang [2]

(b)

while	do while
It is not guaranteed that how many times loop body will get executed.	It is guaranteed that loop body will get executed at-least once.
It is a pre-tested loop.	It is a post–tested loop.

(c) (i) BEST OF LUCK is the correct option. [2]

(d) char check(int n) [2]

(e) (i) boolean   (ii) double [2]

Question 3.

(a) Write a Java expression for the following : $\dfrac{\sqrt{3x + x^2}}{a + b}$ [2]

(b) What is the value of y after evaluating the expression given below ? [2]

y+= ++y + y-- + --y; when int y=8

(c) Give the output of the following : [2]

(i) Math.floor(–4.7)

(ii) Math.ceil(3.4) + Math.pow(2,3)

(d) Write two characteristics of a constructor. [2]

(e) Write the output for the following : [2]

System.out.println ("Incredible"+ "\n"+"world");

(f) Convert the following if else if construct into switch case [2]

```
if (var==1)
     System.out.println ("good");
else if (var==2)
     System.out.println ("better");
elseif (var==3)
     System.out.println ("best");
else
     System.out.println ("invalid");
```

(g) Give the output of the following string functions : [2]

(i) "ACHIEVEMENT".replace('E','A')

(ii) "DEDICATE".compareTo("DEVOTE")

(h) Consider the following String array and give the output [2]

String arr[]= {"DELHI", "CHENNAI", "MUMBAI", "LUCKNOW", "JAIPUR"};

System.out.println (arr[0].length() > arr[3].length());

System.out.print (arr[4].substring(0, 3));

(i) Rewrite the following using ternary operator : [2]

```
     if (bill > 1000)
         discount = bill * 10.0 / 100;
     else
         discount = bill * 5.0 / 100;
```

(j) Give the output of the following program segment and also mention how many times the loop is executed : [2]

```
int i;
   for (i = 5; i > 10; i++)
        System.out.println (i);
        System.out.println ( i * 4 );
```

Answer 3.

(a) Math.sqrt((3 * x) + (x * x))/(a + b);

(b) 33

(c) (i) – 5.0   (ii) 12.0

(d) (i) Constructors have the same name as that of the class.

(ii) They do not have any return type not even void.

(e) Incredible
world

(f) switch(var)

```
{
    case 1: System.out.println ("good");
            break;
    case 2 : System.out.println ("better");
            break;
    case 3 : System.out.println ("best");
            break;
    default : System.out.println ("invalid");
}
```

(g) (i) ACHIAVAMANT

(ii) – 18

(h) false
JAI

(i) discount = bill > 10000 ? (bill * 10.0 / 100) : (bill * 5.0 / 100) ;

(j) Loop will be executed 0 times since the test condition is initially false.
Output will be : 20.

SECTION—B (60 Marks)

*Attempt **any four** questions from this Section.*
*The answers in this Section should consist of the **Programs in either***
Blue J environment or any program environment with Java as the base.
*Each program should be written using **Variable descriptions/Mnemonic***
***Codes** so that the logic of the program is clearly depicted.*
*Flow-Charts and Algorithms **are not required.***

Question 4.

Design a class RailwayTicket with following description :   [15]

Instance variables / data members   :

String name	:	To store the name of the customer
String coach	:	To store the type of coach customer wants to travel
long mobno	:	To store customer's mobile number
int amt	:	To store basic amount of ticket
int totalamt	:	To store the amount to be paid after updating the original amount

Member methods   :

void accept () – To take input for name, coach, mobile number and amount.

void update () – To update the amount as per the coach selected
(extra amount to be added in the amount as follows)

Type of Coaches	Amount
First_AC	700
Second_AC	500
Third_AC	250
Sleeper	None

void display() – To display all details of a customer such as name, coach, total amount and moible number.

Write a main method to create an object of the class and call the above member methods.

Answer 4.

```java
import java.util.*;//importing package
class RailwayTicket
{
String name, coach;
long mobno;
int amt, totalamt;
void accept()
{
    Scanner sc=new Scanner(System.in);
    System.out.println("Enter Details");
    name=sc.nextLine();
    coach=sc.nextLine();
    mobno=sc.nextLong();
    amt=sc.nextInt();
}
void update()
{
    if (coach.equalsIgnoreCase("First_AC"))
    {
        totalamt=amt + 700;
    }
    else if (coach.equalsIgnoreCase("Second_AC"))
    {
        totalamt=amt + 500;
    }
    else if (coach.equalsIgnoreCase("Third_AC"))
    {
        totalamt=amt + 250;
    }
    else if (coach.equalsIgnoreCase("sleeper"))
    {
        totalamt=amt;
    }
}
void display()
{
    System.out.println ("Name : " + name);
    System.out.println ("Coach : " +  coach);
    System.out.println ("Mobile no. : " + mobno);
    System.out.println ("Amt : " + amt);
    System.out.println ("Total Amt : " + totalamt);
}
public static void main(String args[])
{
    RailwayTicket ob = newRailwayTicket();
    ob.accept();//function call
    ob.update();
    ob.display();
}
}
```

Question 5.

Write a program to input a number and check and print whether it is a Pronic number or not. (Pronic number is the number which is the product of two consecutive integers) **[15]**

Example : $12 = 3 \times 4$
$20 = 4 \times 5$
$42 = 6 \times 7$

Answer 5.

```java
import java.util.*;//importing package
class Pronic
{
int n, i = 1, p = 0;
void display()
{
    Scanner sc = newScanner(System.in);
    System.out.println ("Enter a number");
    n=sc.nextInt();
    while (p<=n)
    {
        p=i*(i+1);
        if (p == n)
        {
        System.out.println ("Pronic Number");
        break;
        }//while loop ending
        else if (p>n)
        {
        System.out.println ("Not a Pronic Number");
        break;
        }
        else
        {
        i++;
        }
    }
}
}
```

Question 6.

Write a program in Java to accept a string in lower case and change the first letter of every word to upper case. Display the new string. **[15]**

Sample input : we are in cyber world.

Sample output : We Are In Cyber World.

Answer 6.

```java
import java.util.*;//importing package
class Demo
{
String s,w;
char ch;
int i, l;
void display()
{
    Scanner sc = new Scanner(System.in);
    System.out.println ("Enter a  Sentence");
```

```
        s=sc.nextLine();
        s= s + " ";
        l=s.length();
        for (i=0; i < l; i++)
        {
            w="";
            while (s.charAt(i)!=' ')
            {
            w=w+s.charAt(i);
            i++;
            }//while loop ending
            ch=w.charAt(0);
            ch-=32;
            w=ch + w.substring(1);
            System.out.print (w + " " );
        }
    }
}
```

Question 7.

Design a class to overload a function volume () as follows :   [15]
  (i)   double volume (double R) –with radius (R) as an argument, returns the volume of sphere using the formula.
$$V = 4/3 \times 22/7 \times R^3.$$
  (ii) double volume (double H, double R)–with height(H) and radius(R) as the arguments, returns the volume of a cylinder using the formula.
$$V = 22/7 \times R^2 \times H$$
 (iii) double volume (double L, double B, double H)–with length(L), breadth(B) and Height(H) as the arguments, returns the volume of a cuboid using the formula.
$$V = L \times B \times H$$

Answer 7.

```
class Overload
{// class beginning
double V;
double volume(double R)
{
    V=(4.0/3)*(22/7)*R*R*R);
    return (V);
}
double volume(double H, double R)
{
    V=(22/7)*(R*R)*H;
    return (V);
}
double volume (double L, double B, double H)
{
    V=L*B*H;
    return (V);//returning the value of V
}
}
```

Question 8.

Write a menu driven program to display the pattern as per user's choice.   [15]

Pattern 1	Pattern 2
ABCDE	B
ABCD	LL

```
ABC                 UUU
AB                  EEEE
A
```

For an incorrect option, an appropriate error message should be displayed.

Answer 8.

```java
import java.util.*;//importing package
class Menu
{
int ch, l, i, j;
String s;
public Menu()// constructor
{
s= "";
}
void display()
{
Scanner sc = newScanner(System.in);
System.out.println ("Enter 1 for Pattern1");
System.out.println ("Enter 2 for Pattern2");
ch=sc.nextInt();
if (ch == 1)
{
s="ABCDE";
l=s.length();
for (i = l–1; i >= 0; i– –)
{
for(j = 0; j <= i; j++)
{
    System.out.print (s.charAt(j));
}
System.out.println ();
}
}
else if (ch == 2)
{
s="BLUE";
l=s.length();
for (i = 0; i < l; i++)
{
for (j = 0; j <= i; j++)
{
    System.out.print (s.charAt(i));
}
System.out.println ();
}
}
else
{
System.out.println ("Invalid Choice");
}
}
}
```

Question 9.

Write a program to accept name and total marks of N number of students in two single subscript array name[ ] and totalmarks[ ].   [15]

Calculate and print :

(i) The average of the total marks obtained by N number of students.

  [average = (sum of total marks of all the students)/N]

(ii) Deviation of each student's total marks with the average.

  [deviation = total marks of a student – average]

Answer 9.

```java
import java.util.*;//importing package
class Student
{
int n, i, s=0;
double avg, d;
void display()
{
Scanner sc = new Scanner(System.in);
System.out.println ("Enter number of students");
n=sc.nextInt();
String name[] = new String[n];
int totalmarks[] = new int[n];
for (i = 0; i < n; i++)
{
    System.out.println ("Enter name and total marks");
    name[i] = sc.nextLine();
    totalmarks[i] = sc.nextInt();
    s=s+totalmarks[i];
}
avg=(double)s/n;
System.out.println ("Average = " + avg);
for (i = 0; i < n; i++)
{
    d=totalmarks[i]–avg;
    System.out.println (name[i]  + " Deviation is " + d);
}
}
} // class end
```

MODEL SPECIMEN PAPER–2

SECTION—A

Question 1.
- **(a)** Which operator in Java is used to create an object ?
- **(b)** Define ? : operator.
- **(c)** Write the syntax of do-while loop.
- **(d)** Which library file in Java is used to support input and output data ?
- **(e)** Define ASCII code.

Answer :
- **(a)** new operator.
- **(b)** ? : is a ternary operator. It is also called conditional operator. Its syntax is condition ? expression 1 : expression 2.

  initialization
- **(c)** do

  ```
  {
      body of statements;
      updation
  }
  while (condition);
  ```
- **(d)** java.io is the library file in Java that supports input and output data.
- **(e)** Each character is assigned a specific numeric value in Java called the ASCII code.

Question 2.
- **(a)** Consider the following code

  ```
  int amount = 100;
  while (amount > 0)
  {
      System.out.println (amount);
      amount = amount – 1;
  }
  ```

  Rewrite the above code using
  - (i)   do while loop.
  - (ii) for loop.
- **(b)** Write a class named learning to print "ALL THE BEST FOR YOUR EXAMS".
- **(c)** What will be the output of the following if X = 5 initially
  - (i)   5 * ++X
  - (ii) 5 * X++
- **(d)** If a class is defined as amphibians, give a statement to create an object frog belonging to class amphibians.
- **(e)** How is a character literal represented ?

Answer :
- **(a)** **Using do-while :**

  ```
  int amount = 100;
  {
  do
  {
  System.out.println (amount);
  amount = amount – 1;
  }
  while (amount > 0);
  ```

  Using for :

  ```
  for (int amount = 100; amount > 0; amount —)
  {
  System.out.println (amount);
  }
  ```

(b) class learning
```
{
void main()
{
System.out.println ("ALL THE BEST FOR YOUR EXAMS");
}
}
```
(c) (i) 30

(ii) 25

(d) amphibians frog = new amphibians();

(e) Character literal is represented in single quotes, e.g., 'b'.

Question 3.

(a) Define reserve words. Is catch a reserve word ?

(b) Define function charAt() with an example.

(c) Given the following list of datatypes arrange them in ascending order :

short

int

byte

double

float

long

(d) Define 'this' keyword.

Answer :

(a) Reserve words are those words which are preserved with the system. These cannot be used as variable names. Yes catch is a reserved keyword.

(b) CharAt() returns a character of the string at a particular index

e.g.,   a = "computer";

System.out.println (a.charAt(5));

output = t.

(c) byte

short

int

long

float

double

(d) 'this' keyword is used to refer to the current calling object of the class. It is also used to differentiate between local and global variables when they both have the same name.

SECTION—B

Question 4.

WAP in JAVA to input the basic salary of 10 persons. Each one of them gets 25% of the basic as hra, 15% of the basic as conveyance allowance and 10% of the basic as entertainment allowance. Calculate how many out of 10 got salary above R 5,000 and print the total salary of each person.

Answer :

```
import java.io.*;
class salary
{
        public static void main(String args[]) throws IOException
        {
        double bs[], ca, ent, hra, ts[ ];
```

```
bs = new double [10];
ts = new double [10];
int nm = 0;
int i;
hra = 0;
ca = 0;
ent = 0;
BufferedReader input = new BufferedReader(new InputStreamReader(System.in));
System.out.println ("Enter basic salary");
for (i = 0; i < 10; i++)
{
String n = input.readLine( );
bs[i] = Integer.parseInt(n);
}
for (i = 0; i < 10; i++)
{
hra = 0.25 * bs[i];
ca = 0.15 * bs[i];
ent = 0.10 * bs[i];
ts[i] = bs[i] + hra + ca + ent;
if (ts[i] > 5000)
{
nm ++;
{
System.out.println ("Total Salary" + ts[i]);
}
}
System.out.println ("Number of employees getting more than 5000" + nm);
}
}
```

Question 5.

WAP in Java to find the sum of the following series :

$$1 - \frac{x^2}{2} + \frac{x^3}{3} - \frac{x^4}{4} + \ldots\ldots - \frac{x^n}{N}$$

where $n = 10$ and $x = 2$.

Answer :

```
class series

{
    public static void main()
    {
        int i, j, n, N, x;
        double s;
        n=10;
        x=2;
        s = 1;
        for (i = 2; i <= n; i++)
```

```
        {
            if (i % 2 == 0)
            {
            s = s – Math.pow(x, i)/i;
            }
            else
            {
            s = s + Math.pow(x, i)/i;
            }
        }
        System.out.println ("Sum" + s);
    }
}
```

Question 6.

WAP in Java to accept a string and change each charater of the string in the opposite case and display the new string :

Sample Input Computer Science

Sample Output COMPUTER SCIENCE

Answer :

```java
import java.io.*;
public class check
{
    public static void main(String args[]) throws IOException
    {
        BufferedReader in = new BufferedReader (new InputStreamReader(System.in));
        String name, name1;
        name1 = " ";
        int a, i;
        char chr, chr1;
        chr1 = 0;
        System.out.println ("Enter the word");
        name = in.readLine();
        a = name.length();
        for (i = 0; i < a; i++)
        {
        chr = name.charAt(i);
        if (chr >='A' && chr <='Y' )
        {
        chr1 = Character.toLowerCase(chr);
        name1 = name1 + chr1;
        }
        else if (chr >='a' && chr <= 'Y' )
        {
        chr1 = Character.toUpperCase(chr);
        name1 = name1 + chr1;
        }
        }
        System.out.print (name1);
    }
```

```
}
```

Question 7.

WAP in Java to accept 10 different numbers in a Single Dimensional Array. Arrange them in ascending order using selection sort.

Answer :

```java
import java.io.*;
public class sorting
{
    public static void main(String args[ ]) throws IOException
    {
    BufferedReader in =  (new BufferedReader (new InputStreamReader(System.in));
    int i, j, t;
    int m[ ] = new int [10];
    for (i = 0; i < 10; i++)
        {
        System.out.print ("Enter a no.");
        m [i] = Integer.parseInt (in.readLine ());
        }
    for (i = 0; i < 9; i++)
        {
        for (j = i + 1; j < 10; j++)
            {
            if (m[i] > m[j])
            {
            t = m[i];
            m[i] = m[j];
            m[j] = t;
            }
            }
        }
    System.out.println ("The numbers are");
    for (i = 0; i < 10; i++)
    System.out.println (m[i]);
    }
}
```

Question 8.

Write a program to print the sum of odd digits of an entered number.

Answer :

```java
class prog
{
    public static void main(int n)
    {
        int digit, sum = 0;
        while (n > 0)
        {
            digit = n % 10;
```

```java
        if (digit % 2 != 0)
        sum = sum + digit;
        n = n / 10;
    }
    System.out.println ("The sum of the odd digits is" + sum);
  }
}
```

Question 9.

WAP to input a number and check whether it is palindrome or not.

Answer :

```java
import java.util.*;
class Check
{
    int n, d, t, rev = 0;
    void display()
    {
    Scanner sc = newScanner(System.in);
    System.out.println ("Enter a no.");
    n = sc.nextInt();
    t = n;
    while (n > 0)
    {
        d = n % 10;
        rev = rev * 10 + d;
        n = n / 10;
    }
    if (rev == t)
    {
        System.out.println ("Palindrome No.");
    }
    else
    {
        System.out.println ("Not a Palindrome");
    }
    }
}
```

MODEL SPECIMEN PAPER–3

SECTION—A

Question 1.

(a) What is a constructor ? State the different types of constructors.

(b) What is the purpose of switch statement ?

(c) Define 'BufferedReader' Class.

(d) What is the range for primitive type long ?

(e) What are access specifiers ?

Question 2.

(a) Differentiate between searching and sorting.

(b) Differentiate betwen :

    (i) substring and reverse methods

    (ii) trim and length

    (iii) append and insert

    (iv) compareTo and equals

(c) What will the output of the following code be :

    (i)
```
{
boolean x;
x = ("XYZ" .length() > "ABCD". length()) ? true : false;
System.out.println (x);
}
```

    (ii)
```
{
int m[ ] = {2, 4, 6, 8};
System.out.println (m [1] + " " + m[2]);
}
```

    (iii) Define a class pattern to display the following series :

        1, 4, 9, 16 900

    (iv) Which loop executes atleast once during the execution of the program ?

Question 3.

(a) Define the term loop with an example.

(b) Write down the syntax with reference to Java programming.

    (i) to accept an integral value from the user through console.

    (ii) to accept a fractional number from the user through console.

SECTION—B

Question 4.

Define a class student with the following specifications :

Private members of the class :

admin	Integer
Sname	String type
Eng., Hindi, Math	double
Total	double
ctotal	A function to calculate Eng. + Hindi + Maths with double return type

Takedata() function to accept values and call ctotal() to calculate total marks. Show_data() function to display all the data members on the screen.

Question 5.

WAP to accept monthly salary from the user. Find and display income tax with the help of the following slab :

Monthly Salary	**Income-tax**
8,000 or less	Nil
8,000 – 9000	20% of monthly salary
9,000 – 10000	30% of monthly salary
10,000 or above	40% of monthly salary

Question 6.

WAP to input names and expenses of six departments. Display the names of the departments with highest and lowest expense.

Question 7.

Implement a menu driven program using switch statement in Java that should have the following features :

Addition

Subtraction

Multiply

Division

Modulus

Question 8.

Write a program in Java to accept two numbers and check whether they are twin prime numbers or not.

(Twin prime numbers are those prime numbers whose difference is two).

e.g., (11, 13), (17, 19)

Question 9.

Write a program in Java to accept a string in upper case and find the frequency of each vowel present in the string.

Sample Input : "WE ARE LIVING IN COMPUTER WORLD"

Sample Output : Frequency of   'A' = 1

                               "   "   'E' = 3

                               "   "   'I' = 3

                               "   "   'O' = 2

                               "   "   'U' = 1

MODEL SPECIMEN PAPER–4

SECTION—A

Question 1.
- **(a)** Define tokens.
- **(b)** Define JVM.
- **(c)** What does \f stands for ?
- **(d)** What is the function of length() ?
- **(e)** Define bitwise operator.

Answer :
- **(a)** The smallest individual unit used in a Java statement is known as a token.
- **(b)** Java byte code is excuted by the Java run-time system, which is called Java Virtual Machine (JVM). The Java Virtual Machine or JVM, is an abstract computer that runs compiled Java programs.
- **(c)** \f stands for form feed. It is an escape sequence.
- **(d)** length( ) is used to calculate the length of a string.
- **(e)** An operator that manipulates the contents of variables at the bit level is known as bitwise operator.

  e.g., >> and <<.

Question 2.
- **(a)** Differentiate between

  (i) Parameterized constructors and default constructors.

  (ii) Call by value and call by reference.
- **(b)** Define cascading if-else statement with an example.
- **(c)** Define local variables.
- **(d)** (i) Give the output of the following code :

```
{
int a=0;
int b=10;
a=-b;
System.out.println ("a:"+a+"b:"+b);
}
```

  (ii)
```
{
double w=12.5;
w * = 2;
System.out.println ("w is"+w);
}
```
- **(e)** Define literals ? How many types of literals are supported by Java ?

Answer :

(a) (i)

Parameterized constructors	default constructors
It is a member function with the same name as that of the class name which is used to initialize the object variables by passing parameteric values at the time of its creation.	A constructor which initializes instance variables of an object with definite values readily defined is known as a default constructor.

(ii)

Call by value	Call by reference
A function call whereby the value of the argument passed to the method is the actual value of the data.	A function call whereby the values of the argument passed to the method is a reference to the data rather than the value of the data itself.

(b) Cascading if else statement refers to the structure where there is one or more if statements. It is also known as if-else if-ladder.

e.g. : if (expression 1)

{

if (expression 2)

statement1;

else

statement2;

}

else

{

statement3;

}

(c) **Local variables :** A data item declared within a block, but not accessible to code outside the block is known as a local variable.

(d) (i) a: –10 b : 10

(ii) w is 25.0

(e) Literals refer to the constants used in the program which remain fixed throughout the execution of program.

Types of literals supported by Java are : Integer literals, floating point literal, Character literal, Boolean literal, String literal, Null literal.

Question 3.

(a) Give 2 rules regarding naming a variable.

(b) WAP to print the following format on the screen :

1 2 3 4 5 6 7

1 2 3 4 5

1 2 3

1

Answer :

(a) Two rules regarding naming a variable are :

(i)   A variable name may have any number of characters.

(ii) It should start with alphabet, underscore ('_') or dollar ('$')

(b) class pattern

```
class pattern
{
public static void main()
{
int i, j;
for (i = 7; i >= 1; i = i-2)
{
for (j = 1; j <= i; j++)
System.out.print (j + " ");
System.out.println ( );
}
}
}
```

SECTION—B

Question 4.

WAP in Java to find the temperature in Farenheit when the temperature is given in Celcius.

Answer :

```java
import java.util.*;
class temperature
{
        public static void main()
        {
            double C = 0.0, F = 0.0;
            Scanner sc = new Scanner(System.in);
            System.out.println ("Enter temperature in Celcius");
            C = sc.next Double();
            F = (C/5*9) + 32;
            System.out.println ("Four C = " + C + "F = " + F);
        }
}
```

Question 5.

WAP in Java to accept the sides of a triangle and display whether it is an equilateral or isosceles or scalene triangle.

Answer :

```java
public class triangle
{
public static void main(String args[ ]) throws IOException
{
int a, b, c;
a=0;
b=0;
c=0;
BufferedReader in = new BufferedReader (new InputStreamReader(System.in));
System.out.println ("Enter the three sides of a triangle");
a=Integer.parseInt(in.readLine());
b=Integer.parseInt(in.readLine());
c=Integer.parseInt(in.readLine());
if ((a==b) && (b==c))
    System.out.println ("Equilateral triangle");
else if ((a==b) || (b==c) || (c==a))
    System.out.println ("Isosceles triangle");
else if ((a!=b) && (b!=c) && (c!=a))
System.out.println ("Scalene triangle");
}
}
```

Question 6.

WAP in Java and check whether the number is an Armstrong number or not.

A number is said to be Armstrong, if the sum of the cubes of the digits of the number is equal to the original number.

Eg. : 153 is an armstrong number as $1^3 + 5^3 + 3^3 = 153$

Answer :

```
public class Armstrong
{
public static void main(String args[ ]) throws IOException
{
BufferedReader in = new BufferedReader (new InputStreamReader(System.in));
int n, num, d, s;
s=0;
System.out.println ("Enter your number");
n=Integer.parseInt(in.readLine( ));
num=n;
while (n>0)
{
d=n%10;
s=s+(d*d*d);
n=n/10;
}
if (num==s)
System.out.println ("The number"+num+"is an Armstrong number");
else
System.out.println ("The number" +num+"is not an Armstrong number");
}
}
```

Question 7.

WAP in Java to accept a string and find

(i)   number of blank spaces in the string.

(ii)   number of words in the string.

(iii)   number of characters present in the string.

Answer :

```
import java.io.*;
public class counting
{
public static void main(String args[ ]) throws IOException
{
BufferedReader in = new BufferedReader (new InputStreamReader(System.in));
String name;
int a, i, b, w;
a=0;
b=0;
w=0;
char chr;
chr=0;
```

```
System.out.println ("Enter the string");
name=in.readLine();
a=name.length();
for (i=0; i<a; i++)
{
chr=name.charAt(i);
if (chr=="  ")
b=b+1;
}
w=b+1;
System.out.println ("The no. of blank spaces are "+b);
System.out.println ("The no. of words in the string are "+w);
System.out.println ("The no. of characters are "+(a–b));
}
}
```

Question 8.

WAP in Java to accept a sentence and display the sentence in reversed order of words.

Eg. :   Sample Input : Technology is growing

           Sample output : growing is technology

Answer :

```
import java.io.*;
public class exam
{
public static void main(String args[ ]) throws IOException
{
BufferedReader in = new BufferedReader (new InputStreamReader(System.in));
int sp, ep, l, i, j;
j=0;
String s;
System.out.println ("Enter the string");
s=in.readLine();
s=" "+s;
l=s.length();
ep=l–1;
for (i = l–1; i>=0; i—)
{
if(s.charAt(i) == ' ')
{
    sp=i;
    for (j=sp; j <= ep; j++)
    {
        System.out.print (s.charAt(j));
    }
    ep=sp-1;
}
}
}
}
```

Question 9.

WAP to input ten numbers in an array and print them in ascending order.

Answer :

```java
import java.util.*;
class sort
{
    int A[] = new int [10];
    int i, j, t;
    void display()
    {
        Scanner sc = newScanner(System.in);
        for (i = 0; i < 10; i++)
        {
        System.out.println ("Enter a number");
        A[i] = sc.nextInt();
        }
        for (i = 0; i < 10; i++)
        {
        for (j = i + 1, j < 10; j++)
        {
            if (A[i] > A[j])
            {
                    t  =  A[i];
                A[i]  =  A[j];
                A[j]  =  t;
            }
        }
        }
        for (i = 0; i < 10; i++)
        {
        System.out.println (A[i]);
        }
    }
}
```

MODEL SPECIMEN PAPER–5

SECTION—A

Question 1.

    (a) How are data and functions organized in OOPs ?

    (b) Differentiate between an entry controlled loop and an exit controlled loop.

    (c) Given the following statement :

        final int aint = 500;

        What does the word final signify ?

    (d) What is the purpose of comments in a program ?

    (e) Define operand with an example.

Answer :

    (a) Data, and functions are organised *i.e.,* wrapped up in a single unit which is known as a class.

(b)

Entry Controlled Loop	Exit Controlled Loop
An entry controlled loop is a kind of loop in which there is control on entering the loop. Here, the test expression is evaluated before entering the loop, if it envaluates to true, then the loop is executed otherwise the loop is terminated.	Exist controlled loop is a loop which evaluates its test expression at the end of the loop after executing its loop body statements. It means that an exit controlled loop always executes atleast once, even if the test expression is false initially.
e.g., : for loop, while loop.	*e.g.,* : do-while loop.

    (c) The word final signifies that the value of the variable aint will not change or can never be changed or updated during the program run.

    (d) Comments are used to increase the readability of the program. Comments help the user to understand the program in a better manner as they are self-explanatory. Comments are not executed by the compiler.

    (e) Operand is the entity on which the operator acts.

        e.g.,

$$a + b$$

Operand   operator

Question 2.

    (a) If a function does not returns a result, what will its return type become ?

    (b) Give the output of the following codes

        (i)

```
{
    int totalcost = 6;
    int items = 12;
    System.out.println ("The cost per item is" + (totalcost/items));
}
```

        (ii)

```
{
    int i = 100;
    while (i >= 98)
    {
        System.out.println (i);
        i = i - 1;
    }
}
```

    (c) What is meant by base type of an array ?

    (d) Define character set ?

Answer :

(a) If a function does not returns a result, its return type becomes void.

(b) (i) The cost per item is 0

(ii) 100

99

98

(c) Base type refers to the data type of the array.

(d) Character set is a set of valid characters that a language can recognize.

Question 3.

(a) Define loop control elements.

(b) Given the following expressions

(a) val = 3

(b) val == 3

Answer the following questions.

(i) Are these two statements different ? If yes how ?

(ii) What will be the result of the two statements if the value of val is 5 initially ?

(c) Define escape sequences with an example.

(d) Which OOPs concept provides the principle of reusability ?

(e) Differentiate between base class and derived class.

(f) Suppose, in some situation, it is wanted that the loop body should be executed atleast once, no matter what the initial state of test condition is. Which loop should be used in such a situation ?

(g) Rewrite the following code using ternary operator :

```
{
int c;
if (a > b)
c = a;
else
c = b;
}
```

(h) In a while loop, the loop variable must be updated in which part of the loop ?

Answer :

(a) The elements of a loop which govern the working of the loop are known as loop control elements. The three elements are :

(i) Initialization expression

(ii) Test expression

(iii) Update expression

(b) (i) Yes, the given two statements are totally different. The statement val = 3 is an assignment statement and the statement val == 3 is a relational expression which tests for equality.

(ii) The result of (i) will be val having value 3 and the result of, (ii) will be false because 5 is not equal to 3.

(c) Escape sequences are non-graphic characters represented by a backslash (\) followed by one or more characters.

e.g. : \t — tab space

(d) Inheritance provides the concept of reusability.

(e)

Base class	Derived class
The class whose properties are inherited is known as base class.	The class that inherits the properties is called derived class.

(f) In such a situation, do while loop should be used.

(g) int c = (a > b) ? a : b;

(h) In a while loop, the loop variable must be updated inside the main body of the loop.

SECTION—B

Question 4.

Write a class to print the following format.

```
$
$ $
$ $ $
$ $ $ $
$ $ $ $ $
```

Answer :

```
class format
{
public static void main(String args[ ])
{
    int i, j;
    for (i = 1; i <= 5; i++)
    {
    for (j = 1; j <= i; j++)
    {
        System.out.print ("$');
    }
    System.out.println ( );
    }
}
}
```

Question 5.

U.P. state electricity board charges its consumers according to the following table :

Units Consumed	Call Charges
0 to 200	No Charge
201 to 300	R 1.80/call
301 to 450	R 2.50/call
Above 450	R 3.00/call

The following points have to be kept in mind while calculating the bill :

(1) Monthly rental is R 100.

(2) Free units are upto 200.

WAP in Java to calculate the electricity bill.

Answer :

```
import java.io. *;
class bill
{
public static void main(String args[ ]) throws IOException
{
int u; double charge;
charge = 0.0; u = 0;
BufferedReader in = new BufferedReader (new InputStreamReader(System.in));
System.out.println ("Enter the no. of units");
u = Integer.parseInt(in.readLine( ));
```

```
if (u >= 1 && u <=200)
{
    charge = 100;
}
else if (u > 200 && u <= 300)
{
    charge = 100 + (u – 200) * 1·80;
}
else if (u > 300 && u <= 450)
{
    charge = 100 + (100*1·80) + (4 – 300) * 2·50;
}
else if (u > 450)
{
    charge = 100 + (100 * 1·80) + (150 * 2·50) + (u – 450) * 3·0;
}
System.out.println ("units consumed" + u);
System.out.println ("charge =" + charge);
System.out.println ("additional charge = R 100");
System.out.println ("Total amount =" + charge);
}
}
```

Question 6.

WAP in Java to accept the number of days and display it after converting it into number of years, number of months and no. of remaining days.

Answer:

```
import java.io. *;
public class days
{
public static void main(String args[ ]) throws IOException
{
int a, b, c, y, d;
BufferedReader in = new BufferedReader (new InputStreamReader(System.in));
System.out.println ("Enter the no. of days");
a = Integer.parseInt(in.readLine( ));
y = a / 365;
b = a % 365;
c = b/ 30;
d = b % 30;
System.out.println ("The no. of years =" + y);
System.out.println ("The no. of months =" + c);
System.out.println ("The no. of days =" + d);
}
}
```

Question 7.

(a) WAP in Java to find the sum of the series

$$S = 1 + (1 * 2) + (1 * 2 * 3) + \ldots\ldots 10 \text{ terms}$$

(b) WAP in Java to accept a number and find all its factors (including 1 and excluding the number itself).

Example :

```
Input   : 15
Output  : Factors of 15 = 1, 3, 5
```

Answer :

(a)
```
class series
{
    public static void main( )
    {
        int a, s, p;
            s = 0;
            p = 1;
        for (a = 1; a <= 10; a++)
        {
            p = p * a;
            s = s + p;
        }
        System.out.println ("The sum of the series =" + s);
    }
}
```

(b)
```
import java.io.*;
class factors
{
public static void main(String args[ ] ) throws IOException
{
BufferedReader in = new BufferReader (new InputStreamReader(System.in));
int a, n;
System.out.println ("Enter the no.");
n = Integer.parseInt(in.readLine());
for (a = 2; a < n; a++)
{
if (n % a == 0)
System.out.println (a + "is a factor of" +n);
}
}
}
```

Question 8.

WAP to accept a name (containing three words) and display the initials along with the surname.

e.g. Input : Subhash Chandra Bose

Output : S. C. Bose

Answer :

```
import java.io.*;
class shortform
{
public static void main(String args[ ]) throws IOException
{
BufferedReader in = new BufferedReader (new InputStreamReader(System.in));
int x, y, d;
d = 0;
String a, st;
st ="" "";
char b;
b = '';
System.out.println ("Enter the String");
a = in.readLine();
```

```
x = a.length();
st = st + a.charAt(0);
System.out.println ("The initials along with the surname is");
for (y = 0; y < x; y++)
{
b = a.charAt(y);
if (b == ' ')
{
d = d + 1;
if (d == 1)
st = st + "." + (a.chartAt(y + 1));
if (d == 2)
st = st + "." + (a. substring(y, x));
}
}
System.out.println (st);
}
}
```

Question 9.

WAP in Java to enter a number. Display the sum of the Original number and the reversed number.

e.g.   Original number = 345

                Sum = 888

Answer :

```
import java.io. *;
class sum
{
public static void main(String args[ ]) throws IOException
{
BufferedReader in = new BufferedReader (new InputStreamReader(System.in));
int n, t, rev = 0, d, s;
System.out.println ("Enter a No.");
n = Integer.parseInt(in.readLine());
t = n;
While (t > 0)
{
    d = t % 10;
    rev = rev * 10 + d;
    t = t % 10;
    }
S = n + rev;
System.out.println ("Sum" + S);
}
}
```

MODEL SPECIMEN PAPER–6

SECTION—A

Question 1.

(a) What is Java platform ?

(b) Differentiate between ordinary compilation and Java compilation.

(c) Differentiate between default constructor and parameterised constructor.

(d) Give any two features of Java.

(e) Find the errors in the given program segment.
   Also write the correct statement.

```
Class DVD{
Public int check error (void){
    int X,Y=10;
    X=Y;
    System.out.println ("Result=X", Y)
}}
```

Question 2.

(a) How does Java handle exceptions ?

(b) Mention any two return types of a method with example.

Question 3.

(a) Define sorting. Mention the different types of sorting techniques.

(b) What is constructor ? Explain with an example program.

SECTION—B

Question 4.

Write a program to print rainfall statistics as follows :

This program reads a series of rainfall measurements of a week (number of millimeters of rain, per day). It will then print the following statistics. (Use different functions)

Maximum : The largest amount of rain that fell on any one day of the week.

Average rainfall in a week : Compute this as a floating point number.

For *e.g.* : 1 0 12 7 0 0 11

Output :

Average rainfall = 4.428571428571420

Maximum rainfall = 12.

Question 5.

(a) Write a Java class bank account that is described below

Members	Members name	Description
Member variables	ACnum, ACname ACbalance	Store account number, holder's name and balance.
Default constructor		Initialise AC num, AC name and AC balance.
Parameterised constructor		Initialise AC num, AC name, and AC balance with values accepted from the object.

(b) Write a complete Java program that defines the following methods :

Double()	:	that doubles the balance assigned.
Display()	:	that displays the details.
Main()	:	that calls all the above methods.

Question 6.

(a) Design a class data with 3 data members : day, month and year.

Member method :

(i) Accept date   (ii) Display the date

(b) Write a Java method that extracts first five characters of a string and last five characters of another string. Compare them and print 'EQUAL', if, they match else print 'NOT EQUAL'.

Question 7.

WAP to input three numbers and print them in ascending order.

Question 8.

WAP to input a string and print the frequency of each alphabet present in the string.

Question 9.

WAP to input twelve numbers in ascending order. Input a number and check if it is present in the array or not using binary search technique.

●●

MODEL SPECIMEN PAPER–7

SECTION—A

Question 1.

    (a) What is the difference between 52L and 52 ?

    (b) Define Polymorphism ?

    (c) Write a Java expression for the following expression.

$$x = \frac{-b + (b^2 - 4ac)}{2a}$$

    (d) State the command which prints text on the screen ?

    (e) Define variable.

Answer:

    (a)

52L	52
The constant 52L is of type long.	The constant 52 is of type int.

    (b) A message for an object is interpreted as a request for the execution of a method. The specified method is invoked immediately on receiving the message and the desired results are generated. When the same message is sent to different objects, the interpretation of the message and the response generated will be different. This is termed as Polymorphism.

    (c) d = (b*b) – 4*a*c;

        result = (– b+d)/(2*a);

    (d) System.out.println.

    (e) A variable is a piece of data associated with a class or object. It is a memory location which is used to store any information.

Question 2.

    (a) Is 157A 1 a valid constant ?

    (b) Are commas allowed in constant names ?

    (c) Are blank spaces allowed in variable names ?

    (d) Define array.

Answer :

    (a) No, as constant names do not begin with digits.

    (b) No, as in constant names no special character other than an underscore or dollar sign is allowed.

    (c) No, as in variable names no special character other than an underscore or dollar sign is allowed.

    (d) Arrays are a type of data structure which allows to store a number of values in a single data structure.

Question 3.

    (a) What will be the value of x after evaluating the statement : x = 2 + 3 + 4* 5 + 6 * 7

    (b) Define precedence.

    (c) Write short notes on

        (i) AND operator

        (ii) NOT operator

    (d) If x = 20, y = 10 then determine the result of the following statements

        (i)   x+=y

        (ii) x%=y

        (iii) x*=y

(iv) x–=y

(v) x=y

(e) If a=2, b=5 then what will be the value of x after the execution x = (a>b) ? a:b;

Answer :

(a) x = 2+3+4*5+6*7

x = 2+3+20+42

x = 5+20+42

x = 25+42

x = 67

(b) Precedence is the order in which a program evaluates the operations in a formulae.

(c) **AND Operator :** The AND operator results in true if all the expressions are true.

e.g.: 5>3 && 3<5 : True

NOT Operator :

Logical Not Operator is applied to revert the outcome of an expression.

e.g.: ! (8>3) : false

(d) (i)   30   (ii) 0   (iii) 200

(iv) 10   (v) 10

(e) x=5

SECTION—B

Question 4.

Write a program to find the sum of the following series

$$2\wedge 3 + 3\wedge 3 + 4\wedge 3 \ldots\ldots\ldots\ldots N\wedge 3.$$

Answer :

```
import java.io.*;
import java.lang.*;
class Bluej
{
public static void main(String args[ ]) throws IOException
{
int x=2;
int n;
double c;
c=0;
BufferedReader input = new BufferedReader (new InputStreamReader(System.in));
System.out.println ("Enter value of n");
String V1=input.readLine( );
n=Integer.parseInt(V1);
for (int i=0; i<n; i++)
{
c=c+Math.pow(x, 3);
x++;
}
System.out.println ("Sum of series="+c);
}
}
```

Question 5.

Develop a Java program to find the greatest number out of any 3 numbers using if statements.

Answer :

```java
import java.io.*;
class life
{
public static void main(String args[ ])
{
int a, b, c;
int greatest;
BufferedReader input = new BufferedReader (new InputStreamReader(System in));
System.out.println ("Enter value of a");
String V1=input.readLine();
a=Integer.parseInt(V1);
greatest=a;
System.out.println ("Enter value of b");
String V2=input.readLine( );
b=Integer.parseInt(V2);
if (b > greatest)
greatest=b;
System.out.println ("Enter value of c");
String V3=input.readLine( );
c=Integer.parseInt(V3);
if (c > greatest)
greatest=c;
System.out.println ("Greatest no is"+greatest);
}
}
```

Question 6.

The population of a country is PREP and it increases by 5% every year. The population (PO) of the country after 3 years will be calculated by the formula PO = PREP*1.06* 1.06*1.06.

WAP to calculate the population of the country for three years.

Answer :

```java
import.java.lang.*;
import java.io.*;
public class ever
{
public static void main(int PREP, int time)
{
double x, PO;
x=1.6;
System.out.println ("Present population=" +PREP);
System.out.println ("No. of yrs="+time);
if (time == 1)
{
```

```
PO = PREP*x;
System.out.println ("Population after 1yr="+PO);
}
else
if (time == 2)
{
PO= PREP*x*x;
System.out.println ("Population after two yrs="+PO);
}
if (time == 3)
{
PO= PREP*x*x*x;
System.out.println ("Population after 3 yrs="+PO);
}
}
}
```

Question 7.

WAP in Java to accept a word in lower case and replace the alphabet e, with *.

Sample Input : percentage

Sample Output : p*rc*ntag*

Answer :

```
import java.io.*;
public class replace
{
public static void main(String args[ ]) throws IOException
{
BufferedReader in = new BufferedReader (new InputStreamReader(System.in));
String name;
int l, i, b, w;
l=0;
b=0;
w=0;
char chr;
chr=0;
System.out.println ("Enter String");
name=in.readLine( );
l=name.length( );
for (i=0; i<l; i++)
{
chr=name.charAt(i);
if (chr == 'e')
chr = '*';
System.out.println (chr);
}
}
}
```

Question 8.

Define a class to display the given pattern

```
a
a a
a a a
a a a a
a a a a a
```

Answer :

```
class pattern
{
public static void main( )
{
int i, j;
for (i=1; i <= 5; i++)
{
for (j=1; j <= i; j++)
System.out.print ("a");
System.out.println ( );
}
}
}
```

Question 9.

WAP to display the factorial of any number entered by using while loop.

Answer :

```
class loop
{
public static void main(int n)
{
int i;
double fact;
fact = 1;
i=1;
while (i <= n)
{
fact = fact*i;
i++;
}
System.out.println ("The factorial of the entered number is"+fact);
}
}
```

MODEL SPECIMEN PAPER–8

SECTION—A

Question 1.
- **(a)** Name any two types of Java data types.
- **(b)** Define an identifier. Give an example of the same.
- **(c)** Differentiate between binary search and linear search.
- **(d)** Assign the value of temp = 98.4 to a variable with requisite data type.
- **(e)** Explain switch statement with an example.

Answer :
- **(a)** Two types of datatypes are
    int and float
- **(b)** Identifiers are the basic unit of storage in a Java program.

    e.g. int a;

    Here 'a' is an identifier.
- **(c)**

Binary Search	Linear Search
Binary searching takes place in a sorted array.	Linear searching takes place in an unsorted array.
It is less time consuming.	It is more time consuming.

- **(d)** double temp = 98.8;
- **(e)** Switch statement is a multiway branching statement. It allows many values of an expression to be checked in a single statement. The syntax is :

```
switch (expression)
{
    case value 1 :
            statement;
            break;
    case value 2 :
            statement;
            break;
        default :
            statement;
}
```

e.g.

```
switch (a)
{
case 1 :
        System.out.println ("Yellow");
        break;
case 2 :
        System.out.println ("Blue");
        break;
default :
        System.out.println ("Green");
}
```

Question 2.
- **(a)** Define keywords with an example.
- **(b)** Why do we need a constructor as a class member ?
- **(c)** Explain the term implicit type casting.
- **(d)** Name the following :
    - (i) A package that is invoked by default.
    - (ii) A keyword to use the classes defined in a package.
- **(e)** Name the class that is used for different mathematical functions. Give an example of a mathematical function.

Answer :
    (a) The words which convey a special meaning to the compiler and cannot be used as variable names are known as keywords or reserve words.
        e.g. : default, break, etc.
    (b) A constructor is used to set initial state of an object. It is executed automatically at the time of creation of object.
    (c) Implicit type casting refers to the type conversion which is done automatically by the compiler itself.
    (d) (i) java.lang
        (ii) import
    (e) Math is the class which is used to perform different mathematical functions.
        e.g. : abs(), sqrt ().

Question 3.
    (a) State the meaning of != and ==.
    (b) Write an equivalent Java syntax for the following expression a = 0.05 - 2y3.
    (c) Rewrite the following using conditional assignment operator if(income <= 1000)
        tax=0;
        else
        tax=12;
    (d) Write a statement for each of the following
        (i)   Store a number 800 as string.
        (ii)   Convert the string into a numeric value.
        (iii)   Add it to the existing total of 1000 to update the SUM.
    (e) (i)   What is the role of the keyword void in declaring functions ?
        (ii)   If a function contains several return statements, how many of them will be executed ?
        (iii)   Which OOP principle implements DATA HIDING ?
    (f) What is the output of the following :
        System.out.println ("FIVE:"+5+2);
        System.out.println ("SIX:"+(5+2));
    (g) Evaluate the following expressions, if the values of the variables are a=1, b=3 and c=4.
        (i) a++ + b++ + c--
        (ii) a-- + b++ + a.

Answer :
    (a) != refers to not equal to and == refers to equal to.
    (b) double a = (0.05 – 2*Math.pow(y,3));
    (c) int tax = (income <= 1000)? 0 : 12;
    (d) (i)   String S;
                S = "800";
        (ii)   int n = Integer.parseInt(S);
        (iii)   int sum;
                total = 1000;
                sum = total+n;
    (e) (i)   void means no datatype. In a function it is used to declare that the function will not return any value.
        (ii)   Only one *i.e.*, the first one.
        (iii)   Encapsulation.
    (f) FIVE:52
        SIX:7
    (g) (i) a++ + b++ + c--
             = 1+3+4
             = 8
        (ii) a-- + b++ + a
             = 1+3+0
             = 4

SECTION—B

Question 4.

WAP to convert a given temperature from Farenheit to Celsius or *vice-versa*. Give user choice to choose an option.

Answer :

```java
import java.io.*;
class temp
{
    private double C, F;
    public void temp( ) throws IOException
    {
    char ch= ' ';
    int num = 0;
    double C, F;
    BufferedReader br = newBufferedReader (new InputStreamReader(System.in));
    BufferedReader br1 = new BufferedReader (new InputStreamReader(System.in));
    System.out.println("1. Farenheit to Celsius");
    System.out.println("2. Celsius to Farenheit");
    System.out.println("Enter choice");
    ch=(char)br.read();
    if (ch == '1')
    {
    System.out.println ("Enter temperature.in Farenheit");
    String result= br.readLine( );
    num = Integer.parseInt(result);
    C = (num-32)/1.8;
    System.out.println ("Temperature in Celsius" +C);
    }
    else
    {
    System.out.println ("Enter temperature in Celsius");
    String result = br1.readLine( );
    num = Integer.parseInt(result);
    F = 1.8*num+32;
    System.out.println ("Temperature in Farenheit"+F):
    }
    }
}
```

Question 5.

Write a program to compute and display the sum of the following series :
$S=1+1/2+1/3----+1/10$.

Answer :

```java
class series
{
public static void main( )
{
int a;
double s;
```

```
s=0;
for (a=1; a <= 10; a++)
s = s +1/a;
System.out.println ("The sum is"+s);
}
}
```

Question 6.

WAP to generate the first n terms of fibonacci series.

Answer :

```
class Fibonacci
{
public static void main()
{
System.out.print (a+" "+b);
int a=0, b=1, c;
for(int j = 3; j <= n; j++)
{
c = a+b;
System.out.print (c+ " ");
a=b;
b=c;
}
}
}
```

Question 7.

WAP that accepts numbers and displays whether the number is odd or even. Accept numbers till the user enters zero.

Answer :

```
import java.io.*:
class nopublic
{
public void check() throws IOException
{
BufferedReader br = new BufferedReader (new InputStreamReader(System.in));
int num;
String str;
System.out.println ("Enter zero to quit");
do
{
str = br.readLine( );
num = Integer.parseInt(str);
if (num % 2 == 0)
System.out.println ("Even");
else
System.out.println ("odd");
}while (num != 0);
}
}
```

Question 8.

WAP to accept 10 names and display them in uppercase.

Answer :

```java
import java.io.*;
public class Arrdemo
{
String [ ] anArray = new String [10];
String str;
public void accept() throws IOException
{
BufferedReader bReader = new BufferedReader (new InputStreamReader(System.in));
for (int i = 0; i < anArray.length; i++)
{
    System.out.println ("Enter a number");
    str=bReader.readLine( );
    anArray[i]=str;
}
for (int j = 0; j < anArray.length; j++)
{
    System.out.println ("Name" +j+ ":" + anArray[j].toUpperCase());
}
}
}
```

Question 9.

WAP that reverses a number passed as a parameter. It should also display the sum of all the digits present in the number.

Answer :

```java
class demo
{
public static void main(int n)
{
int rem, sum=0, rev=0;
while (num > 0)
{
  rem  =  num % 10;
   rev  =  rev * 10+rem:
  sum  =  sum+rem;
 num  =  num / 10;
}
System.out.println ("The reverse is" + rev);
System.out.println ("The sum is" +sum);
}
}
```

MODEL SPECIMEN PAPER–9

SECTION—A

Question 1.

Differentiate between.

(a) if-else and switch case statements.

(b) while and do-while loops.

(c) byte datatype and short datatype.

(d) tab and new line.

(e) ceil() and floor().

Question 2.

(a) What is the range of a float datatype ?

(b) Define ternary operator with an example.

(c) Why is break statement used in a switch case statement ?

(d) Name the function of Java which is used to remove all the white spaces at the beginning and at the end of a string.

(e) Give the syntax of declaring a string in Java.

(f) Define constructors.

(g) Give the output of the following code

```
{
    int a = 0, b = 30, c = 40;
    a – = b + c + ++b;
    System.out.println ("a is equal to" + a);
}
```

(h) If a = 2, b = 0, c = 3; what will be the value of a, b and c after the following statement executes :

```
if (c == 3)
b = 5;
else
a = 3;
```

(i) Is it possible to use a continue statement in a switch case statement ?

(ii) Give two rules for writing variable names in Java.

Question 3.

(a) What is the difference between int i, and double i.

(b) When two mathematical operations have the same precedence, how is the operation performed ?

(c) Name the relational operators supported by Java.

SECTION—B

Question 4.

Define a class pattern which takes an integer argument and prints the following pattern as shown in the example :

for n = 3

the pattern would be :

```
        1
      1 2 1
    1 2 3 2 1
      1 2 1
        1
```

Question 5.

WAP to input seven numbers in an array and print the position of the smallest element of the array.

Question 6.

WAP to print all prime numbers between 100 and 700 using do while statement.

Question 7.

WAP to enter a string and print the characters of the string present at even positions.

e.g.,

Input : India is my country

Output : The characters of the string at even positions are : niimcuty.

Question 8.

A class named as 'Result' has three data members *viz.,* Name, Roll no. and percentage. The grades are assigned on the following criteria :

Percentage	Grade
90% and above	A +
80% - 89%	A
70% - 79%	B
60% - 69%	C
50% - 59%	D

WAP to declare the class Result and print the grades accordingly.

Question 9.

WAP to print the sum of the following series :

$$S = a/1 + a/2 + a/3 \ldots\ldots\ldots\ldots + a/n$$

where a and n are inputs from the user.

MODEL SPECIMEN PAPER–10

SECTION—A

Question 1.

(a) In Java, strings are concatenated using which kind of operator ?

(b) Which library file in Java is used for basic runtime support for Java ?

(c) Define subscript ?

(d) If a division is performed with integer operands, by default Java will return which kind of value ?

(e) Define unary operator with an example.

Answer :

(a) In Java concatenation operator is +.

(b) java.lang is the library file in Java that is used for basis runtime support for Java.

(c) A symbol or a number used to identify an individual element within an array is known as subscript.

(d) By default it will return integer value.

(e) An arithmetic operator, which is appplied with a single operand is known as unary operator, *e.g.* : ++, – –

Question 2.

(a) Consider the following statements :

public static void main(String args[ ])

what do the following words stand for :

(i)   public

(ii)   static

(iii)   void

(iv)   main

(b) Evaluate the following expressions :

When int a = 10, b = 8;

(i)   a % b++

(ii)   ++a – b––

(iii)   a++ – b––

(iv)   a–– + b++

(c) Define type conversion.

(d) What will be the output of the following code :

```
{
    int num = 30,
    num + = 100,
    system.out.println (num);
    num – = 10;
    system.out.println (num);
    num / = 3;
    system.out.println (num);
    num * = 4,
    system.out.println (num);
    num % = 9,
    system.out.println (num);
}
```

Answer :

(a) (i) public : It stands for the access specifier which declares the main function to be publically accessible to all other classes.

(ii) static : It declares that every function or method is independent of the entire class and does not figure as a part of any objects of the class.

(iii) void : It is a data type modifier which defines the main function is of no return type.

(iv) main : It refers to the name of the function.

(b) (i) 2

(ii) 3

(iii) 2

(iv) 8

(c) In a mixed expression, the result can be obtained in any form of its data types. Hence, it is needed to convert the various data types into a single type. It is known as type conversion.

(d) 130

120

40

160

7

Question 3.

(a) Differentiate between the following with examples.

(i) Local and global variables.

(ii) Prefix and postfix operators.

(b) Which of the following answers does the same thing as following :

value + = sum++;

(i) value = value + sum;

sum = sum + 1,

(ii) sum = sum + 1,

value = value + sum,

(iii) value = value + sum

(iv) value = value++ + sum

Answer :

(a) (i)

Local Variables	Global Variables
These are those variables that are declared with the body of a method and are available only within the method.	These are declared outside any method. The scope of such variables is till the end of the program.

(ii)

Postfix Operation	Postfix Operation
When increment or decrement operators are applied before the operand, it is known as prefix operators. These work on the principles of change before action.	When increment or decrement operators are used after the operand, it is known as postfix operator.

(b) (i) Is the correct answer.

SECTION—B

Question 4.

WAP to bubble sort the following set of values in ascending order :

5, 3, 8, 4, 9, 2, 1, 12, 98, 16

Answer :

```
class test
{
public static void main()
{
int i, j;
int a[] = {5, 3, 8, 4, 9, 2, 1, 12, 98, 16};
int l = a.length;
for (int i = 0; i < l; i++)
{
for (int j = 0; j < l - 1 - i; j++)
if (a[j] > a[j + 1])
{
int t = a[j];
a[j] = a[j + 1];
a[j+ 1] = t;
}
}
System.out.println ("The sorted array is:");
for (int i = 0; i<1; i++)
{
System.out.println (a[i]);
}
}
}
```

Question 5.

WAP to calculate the commission of a salesman of books, as per the following table :

Sales	Commission
More than and Equal to R	25%
R 80,000 to 99,999	22.5%
R 60,000 to R 79,999	20%
R 40,000 to R 59,999	15%
Less than 40,000	12.5%

Answer :

```
import java.io.*;
public class commission
{
public static void main(String args[ ]) throws IOException
{
double sales;
double comm;
comm = 0;
sales = 0;
BufferedReader in = new BufferedReader (new InputStreamReader(System.in));
```

```
System.out.println ("Enter the value of sales");
sales = Double.parseDouble(in.readLine());
if (sales > 100000)
{
    comm = sales * (0.25);
    System.out.println ("Commission" + comm);
}
else
if (sales >= 60000)
{
    comm = sales * (0.20);
    System.out.println ("Commission" + comm);
}
else
if (sales >= 40000)
{
    comm = sales * (0.15);
    System.out.println ("Commission" + comm);
}
else
{
    comm = sales * (0.125);
    System.out.println ("Commission" + comm);
}
}
}
```

Question 6.

Define an array of size 12. Write a program which accepts elements from the keyboard and finds the sum of the entered numbers and also prints the odd number entered from the keyboard.

Answer :

```
import.java.util.*;
Class Demo
{
    int A[ ] = new int [12];
    int i, s = 0;
    void display( );
    {
        Scanner sc = new Scanner(Sysem.in);
        for (i = 0; i < 12; i++)
        {
            System.out.println ("Enter a number");
            A[i] = sc.nextInt( );
        }
        for (i = 0; i < 12; i++)
        {
            S = S + A[i];
            if ((A[i] / 2 ) != 0)
```

```
            {
                System.out.println (A[i]);
            }
        }
        System.out.println ("Sum is" + S);
    }
}
```

Question 7.

Write a program to assign 10 different numbers in a single dimensional array and display the greatest number.

Answer :

```
public class array
{
public static void main(String args[ ])
{
int i, max;
max = 0;
int m[]={12, 34, 23, 7, 14, 65, 67, 81, 23, 77);
for (i = 0; i < 10; i++)
{
if (max < m[i])
    max = m[i];
}
System.out.println ("The greatest element =" + max);
}
}
```

Question 8.

WAP in Java to print the following pattern :

```
        a
       a a
      a a a
     a a a a
    a a a a a
```

Answer :

```
public class pattern
{
public static void main(String args[ ])
{
int i, j, k, m;
m = 4;
for (j = 1; 1 <= 5; i++)
{
for (j = 1; j <= m; j++)
System.out.print (" ");
for (k = 1; k <= i; k++)
System.out.print ("a");
System.out.println ();
m = m–1;
}
}
}
```

Question 9.

WAP to input a string and print the consecutive pairs of vowels present in it.

Answer:

```java
import java.util.*;
class vowels
{
    String s;
    int i, l;
    char ch, ch2;
    void display( )
    {
        Scanner sc = new Scanner(System.in);
        System.out.println ("Enter a String");
        s = sc.nextLine( );
        l = s.length( );
        s = s.toLowerCase( );
        for (i = 0; i < l – 1; i++)
        {
            ch = s.charAt(i);
            ch2 = s.charAt(i+1);
            if ((ch == 'a'|| ch == 'e'|| ch =='i'|| ch =='o' ||
            ch =='u') && (ch2 == 'a'|| ch2 =='e' || ch2 =='i' ||
            ch2 == '0' || ch2 == 'u'))
            {
                System.out.println (ch+" "ch2);
            }
        }
    }
}
```

MODEL SPECIMEN PAPER–11

SECTION—A

Question 1.

   (a) Define encapsulation.

   (b) Explain the term object using an example.

   (c) Define a variable.

   (d) What is a wrapper class ? Give an example.

   (e) What is the purpose of the new operator ?

Answer :

   (a) Encapsulation is one of the core concepts of Object Oriented Programming. It is the binding or the wrapping up of variables and functions.

   (b) An object is an instance of a class. *e.g.* : Car, TV are the instances of the class automobile and electronics.

   (c) A variable is a memory location by a particular name.

   (d) Wrapper class is used to convert String objects into primitive data types and *vice-versa. e.g.,* Integer, Character, Double, Float etc. examples could be integer, character etc.

   (e) A new operator is used to allocate memory to a newly created object or any array.

Question 2.

   (a) State the two kinds of data types.

   (b) Write the corresponding Java expressions for the following mathematical operations :

      (i) $a^2 + b^2$

      (ii) $z = x^3 + y^3 - xy/z$

      (iii) Define an impure function.

      (iv) Differentiate between if and switch statements.

      (v)   What will be the output for the following program segment ?

```
String s = new String("abc");
System.out.println (s.toUpperCase());
```

Answer :

   (a) The two kinds of data types are :

      (i)   Primitive data types.   (ii)   Non-primitive data types.

   (b) (i)   Math.pow(a,2) + Math.pow(b,2);

      (ii) z = Math.pow(x,3) + Math.pow(y,3) – (x * y)/z;

      (iii) An impure function is a function which changes the state of an object received through parameters.

      (iv)

Switch Statement	If Statement
Switch accepts only int or character data types.	If accepts any data type accordingly.
Switch statement supports equality.	If statement supports all other relations accordingly.

      (v) ABC

Question 3.

   (a) What is meant by private visibility of a method ?

   (b) Find and correct the errors in the following program segment.

```
int n[ ]=(2,4,6,8,10);
for (int i=0; i<=5; i++)
System.out.println (n["+i+"1 + n[i]);
```

(c) Explain function overloading with an example.

(d) Find the output of the following program segment, when

    (i) val = 500   (ii) val = 1600

```
int val, sum, n=550;
sum = n+val >1750 ? 400 : 200;
System.out.println (sum);
```

(e) What is a default constructor ?

(f) What will be the output for the following program segment ?

```
int a=0, b=30, c=40;
a= --b + c++ + b;
System.out.println ("a="+a);
```

(g) Differentiate between compareTo() and equals() methods.

(h) What is a package ? Give an example.

(i) Explain the function of a return statement.

Answer :

(a) The private visibility of a method means that the method cannot be accessed outside the class.

(b)
```
int n[ ]={2,4,6,8,10};
for(int i=0; i<5; i++)
System.out.println ("n ["+i+"] "+n [i] );
```

(c) In Java two or more functions can be defined within the same class that share the same name but differ in the number and/or types of arguments. These functions are said to be overloaded and the process is referred to as function overloading.

```
class worktodo
worktodo(int a, int b);
worktodo(int a);
worktodo()
```

(d) (i)   200

    (ii) 400

  if precedence is not considered

    (i)   750

    (ii) 750.

(e) A default constructor has no arguments, it has the same name as that of the class and is used to initialize instance variables with default values.

(f) a=99

(g)

compareTo()	equals()
compareTo() method is used to check less than or greater than conditions.	equals() method is only used to check equality.

(h) A package is a collection of related types providing access protection and name space management.

Example : io, lang, util, etc.

(i) The return statement returns a value to the calling method within the program. It is also used to terminate the execution of a function.

SECTION—B

Question 4.

Write a program to calculate and print the sum of odd numbers and the sum of even numbers for the first n natural numbers. The integer n is to be entered by the user.

Answer :

```
class numbers
{
    int sumeven=0;
    int sumodd=0;
    public void work(int n)
    {
    for (int i = 1 ; i <= n; i++)
    {
        if (i%2 == 0)
        sumeven = sumeven+i;
        else
        sumodd = sumodd+i;
    }
    System.out.println ("Sum of odd numbers is"+sumodd);
    System.out.println ("Sum of even numbers is "+sumeven);
    }
}
```

Question 5.

A cloth showroom has announced the following festival discounts on the purchase of items, based on the total cost of the items purchased :

Total Cost	Discount (in Percentage)
Less than R 2000	5%
R 2001 to R 5000	25%
R 5001 to 10000	35%
Above R 10000	50%

Write a program to input the total cost and to compute and display the amount to be paid by the customer after availing the discount.

Answer :

```
class abed
{
    public void check(int totalcost)
    {
        double cost=0, amount=0, discount=0;
        if (totalcost <= 2000)
        discount = 5:
        else if (totalcost <= 5000)
        discount = 25;
        else if (totalcost < 10000)
        discount = 35;
        else
        discount = 50;
        amount = totalcost – (totalcost*discount /100);
        System.out.println (The amount being paid by the customer is"+amount);
    }
}
```

Question 6.

Consider the following statement :

"January 26 is celebrated as the Republic Day of India".

Write a program to change 26 to 15, January to August, Republic to Independence and finally print "August 15 is celebrated as the Independence Day of India".

Answer :

```
public class replace
{
public void convert()
{
String str="26 January is celebrated as republic day:";
String sent="";
String newstring = "";
int len=str.length();
for (int i = 0; i< len; i++)
{
char b=str.charAt(i); //extract characters
if (b != ' ')//till we do not get a space add characters to sent
sent = sent+b;
else
{ //compare the word extracted with the words to be changed
int c=sent.compareTo("26");
int d=sent.compareTo("Republic");
int e=sent.compareTo("January");
if (c==0) //if the word exists replace it with the given words
    newstring=newstring+" "+"15";
else if (d==0)
    newstring=newstring+" "+"Independence";
else if (e==0)
    newstring+="August";
else //otherwise add the word as it is to newstring
    newstring+=" "+sent;
sent="";
}
}
System.out.println (newstring);
}
}
```

Question 7.

Write a program that outputs the results of the following evaluations based on the number entered by the user :

(i)   Natural Logarithm of the number.

(ii)   Absolute value of the number.

(iii) Square root of the number.

(iv)   Random numbers between 0 and 1.

Answer :

```
class random
    {
    public void numbers( )
```

```
{
System.out.println ("1. Natural Logarithm");
System.out.println ("2. Absolute Value");
System.out.println ("3. Square Root");
System.out.println ("4. Random Numbers between 0-1"):
System.out.println ("Enter choice and a number");
}
public void calculate(int choice, double number)
{
double n;
switch (choice)
{
case 1 :  n = Math.log(number);
          System.out.println ("The result is"+n);
          break;
case 2 :  n = Math.abs(number);
          System.out.println ("The result is "+n);
          break;
case 3 :  n = Math.sqrt(number);
          System.out.println ("The result is "+n);
          break;
case 4 :  n = Math.random( );
          System.out.println ("The result is "+n);
          break;
}
}
}
```

Question 8.

The marks obtained by 50 students in a subject are tabulated as follows :

Name	Marks
*	*
*	*

Write a program to input the names and marks of the students in the subject.

Calculate and display :

(i)   The subject average marks (subject average marks = subject total/50)

(ii) The highest mark in the subject and the name of the student. (The maximum marks in the subject are 100)

Answer :

```
class highest
{
//enter name and percentage of 50 children.
String n;
int high=0; // To store the highest percentage.
public void calculate(String nam[ ], int perc[])
{
for (int i = 0; i < perc.length; i++)
{
//To find the highest percentage and similarly store the name
//in N.
```

```
if (perc[i] > high)
{
high=perc[i];
n=nam[i];
}
}
System.out.println ("highest percentage :"+high);
System.out.println ("name of the child :"+n);
}
}
```

Question 9.

Write a program to accept 15 integers from the keyboard, assuming that no integer entered is zero. Perform selection sort on the integers and then print them in ascending order.

Answer :

```
class array
    {// input 15 integers
    public void compute(int a[ ])
    {
    //selection sorting
    for (int t = 0; i < a.length-1; i++)
    {
        for (int j = i+1; j < a.length; j++)
        {
        if (a[i] > a[j])
        {
                int t  =  a[i];
                 a[i]  =  a[j];
                 a[j]  =  t;
        }
        }
    }
//display
for (int i = 0; i < a.length; i++)
System.out.println (a[i]);
}
}
```

MODEL SPECIMEN PAPER–12

SECTION—A

Question 1.
  (a) Define operators.
  (b) What is a data type ? Give an example.
  (c) Define empty loop with an example.
  (d) Can arrays be initialised before declaring them ?
  (e) Define data abstraction.

Question 2.
  (a) Define a block with an example.
  (b) Name the kind of searching in which the middle position of the array is examined first.
  (c) How is a statement terminated in Java ?
  (d) What is meant by nested for loop ?
  (e) Name any four typs of tokens in Java.

Question 3.
  (a) Concantenate the following two strings to get the string "Feel Fresh".
       String a = "Feel";
       String b = "Fresh";
  (b) Give the output of the following codes :
       (i)
```
int f=1, i=2;
do
{
    f*=i;
    i++;
}   while (i < 5);
System.out.println (f);
```
       (ii)
```
int a=0, P=1;
for (int i = 1; i < 5; i++)
{
    a=a+p*i;
    System.out.println (a);
}
```
       (iii) Assume the following :
```
String s, t, h, a;
String n, e,
int i;
h = "Hello";
S = "How are you ?";
a = "abc";
n = "null";
e = "            SUM            ";
```
       Give the values of the following expressions :
       (i)   a.length()
       (ii)   n.substring(1)
       (iii) h.indexOf("H")
       (iv)   s.substring(1, 3)
       (v)   e.trim() + n;

(c) Differentiate between indexOf() and lastindexOf().

(d) Differentiate between private and public visibility labels.

(e) Define bubble sort.

SECTION—B

Question 4.

WAP to input ten numbers in an array and print the sum of the largest and the smallest number present in it.

Question 5.

Write a class convert which takes an argument representing currency in Rupees and convert it into paisa.

Question 6.

Write a program using string function to input any word and print the same in alphabetical order.

Question 7.

Write a program to calculate the charges of a telegram bill according to the following tariff : Upto 10 words, charge is R 3.00 and .40 per word additional.

Question 8.

Write a program to calculate the sum of the following series :

S = 1 – 2 + 3 – 4 + ………….. N terms

Where N is input.

Question 9.

Define a class with a number function to accept the monthly salary from the user and display income tax according to the following rules :

Monthly Salary	Income Tax
9,000 or more	40% of monthly salary
7,500 to 8999	30% " "
7,499 or less	20% " "

●●

MODEL SPECIMEN PAPER–13

SECTION—A

Question 1.
- (a) Define selection sort.
- (b) Double precision uses how many bits to store a value ?
- (c) Define an expression.
- (d) What is meant by dynamic initialization ?
- (e) Define relational operators.

Answer :
- (a) In selection sorting, successive rounds are executed to select the elements in some order and place them in their positions.
- (b) Double precision uses 64 bits to store a value.
- (c) A combination of operands and operators that produces a resulting value is known as an expression.
- (d) Initialization of variables during run time is known as dynamic initialization.
- (e) Relational operators are used to show relationship among the operands
  e.g. : $<, >, <=, >$

Question 2.
- (a) If $y = 14$, then find $z = (++y * (y++ + 5))$
- (b) What will be the output, if the following statement is executed int x = 90;
  char c = (x <= 90) ? 'z' : '10';
- (c) In an expression, if two operators have the same precedence. Which will be performed first ?
- (d) Define if statement.

Answer :
- (a) $z = (++y * (y++ + 5))$
  $z = (15 * (15 + 5))$
  $z = (15 * (20))$
  $z = 300$
- (b) c ='z'
- (c) The operator at the left hand side will be performed first.
- (d) If condition is used to check a specific condition. It performs a course of action if the condition is true, otherwise it is ignored.

Question 3.
- (a) Differentiate between if else and switch case statement.
- (b) Rewrite the following code using ternary operator.

```
{
    if (a != b)
        c = a;
    else
        c = b;
}
```

- (c) consider the following statement :
```
for (; a <= 5; a++)
{
    body of the loop
}
```
will this loop work ? If yes, how.

- (d) What will be the output of the following code :
```
class series
{
public static void main()
```

```
{
int a, j;
for (a = 1; a <= 7; a++)
{
for (j = 1; j < a; j++)
System.out.println (a + " ");
System.out.println ( );
}
}
}
```

(e) What is the need of using a wrapper class ?

(f) Define package.

Answer :

(a)

If Else	Switch Case
1. It results in boolean type values.	It results in integer type values.
2. Does not uses break statement.	Uses break statement.
3. No default operation.	Default operation is present.

(b) c = (a != b)? a : b;

(c) Yes, this loop will work. It will start with a garbage, initial value and operates the loop body unless the test condition is false.

(d) 1

2 2

3 3 3

4 4 4 4

5 5 5 5 5

6 6 6 6 6 6

7 7 7 7 7 7 7

(e) Wrapper classes are needed for the following functions :

    (i)   The primitive values can be stored in objects.

    (ii) To provide conversion system form character / string type to other types.

(f) A package is a group of classes, which can be imported to a program so that the user may exercise the methods and functions available in it.

SECTION—B

Question 4.

The production (P) of crude oil of a country in millions of barrels may be estimated by the following set of instructions

$$P = 5 + 3t, \ 0 < t <= 3$$
$$P = 14 + (t - 5/2), \text{ for } t > 3$$

WAP in Java to find the quantity of production for every year t = 1 to 10 and print it.

Answer :

```
class oil
{
public static void main()
{
int t, p;
for (t = 1; t <= 10; t++)
{
```

```
    if (t <= 3)
        P = 5 + 3 * t;
    else
        P = 14 + (t – 5 / 2);
    }
    System.out.println ("production of" + (t + 1) + "years =" +p+ "gallons");
    }
}
```

Question 5.

WAP to compute the middle digit of any entered number. If the no. does not have a middle digit, it has to return the average of the middle two digits.

Answer :

```
class number
{
int nthno(int m, int n)
{
int a[ ] = new int [100];
int b[ ] = new int [100];
int x, mm, i = 0;
mm = m;
while (mm != 0)
{
    i = i + 1;
    x = mm % 10;
    a[i] = x;
    mm = mm / 10;
}
for (int j = 0; j < i; j++)
{
    b[j] = a[i – j];
}
x = b[n];
return(x);
}
void input number(int m)
{
int z, S, c = 0;
z = m*;
while (z != 0)
{
z = z / 10;
c = c + 1;
if ((c % 2) == 0)
{
    int S1, S2;
    S1 = (1, (c + 2)/2);
    S = (S1 + S2)/2;
}
```

```
else
{
S = nthno*** (m, (c + 1)/2);
}
}
System.out.println ("Middle term is" + S);
}
}
```

Question 6.

Write a class display to print the following format

```
5   5   5   5   5
5   4   4   4   4
5   4   3   3   3
5   4   3   2   2
5   4   3   2   1
```

Answer :

```
class summation
{
public static void main()
{
int a = 5, e = 5;
for (int i = 5; i >= 1; i--)
{
    for (int k = a; k >= i; k--)
    {
        System.out.print (k);
    }
    for (int j = 1; j <= c - 1; j++)
    {
        System.out.print (c);
    }
    System.out.println ();
    c = c - 1;
}
}
}
```

Question 7.

WAP in Java to accept a string and count the number of vowels present in the string
Sample Input : Computer Applications
Sample Output : The number of vowels = 8

Answer :

```
import java.io.*;
public class vowels
{
public static void main(String args[]) throws IOException
{
BufferedReader in = new BufferedReader (new InputStreamReader(System. in));
int x, y, v;
```

```
v=0;
String a;
char b;
System.out.println ("Enter your string");
a = in.readLine();
x = a.length();
for (y = 0; y < x; y++)
{
    b = (a.charAt(y));
    if ((b == 'a') || (b == 'e') || (b == 'i') || (b == 'o') ||
    (b == 'u') || (b == 'A') || (b == 'E') || (b == 'I')
    (b == 'O') || (b == 'U'))
        v = v+ 1;
}
System.out.println ("The no. of vowels in the string =" + v);
}
}
```

Question 8.

WAP to input names of ten students. Input a name and check whether it is present in the list or not.

Answer :

```
import java.util.*;
class Search
{
    String A[ ]= new String [10];
    String S;
    int i, flag = 0;
    void display( )
    {
        Scanner sc = new Scanner(System.in);
        for (i = 0; i < 10; i++)
        {
            System.out.println ("Enter a name");
            A[i] = sc.nextLine( );
        }
        System.out.println ("Enter the name to be searched");
        s=sc.nextLine( );
        for (i = 0; i < 10; i++)
        {
            if (s.equalsIgnoreCase(A[i]))
            {
                flag = 1;
                break;
            }
        }
        if (flag == 1)
            System.out.println ("Found");
        else
            System.out.println ("Not Found");
    }
}
```

Question 9.

WAP to input a string and check whether it is palindrome or not.

Answer :

```java
import java.util.*;
Class Pallin
{
    String s,rev = "";
    int i, l;
    void display( )
    {
        Scanner sc = new Scanner(System.in);
        System.out.println ("Enter a string");
        s=sc.next( );
        l=s.length( );
        for (i = l – 1; i >= 0; i– –)
        {
            rev = rev + s.charAt(i);
        }
        if (s.equalsIgnoreCase(rev))
        {
            System.out.println ("Palindrome");
        }
        else
        {
            System.out.println ("Not a Palindrome");
        }
    }
}
```

MODEL SPECIMEN PAPER–14

SECTION—A

Question 1.
- **(a)** Which element is num[9] of the array num ?
- **(b)** What is an infinite loop ?
- **(c)** If there is no test expression in a for loop, how many times the loop will execute.
- **(d)** What is the process of calling a function in such a way that the change in formal arguments reflects in actual parameters known as ?
- **(e)** Define Iteration ?

Answer :
- **(a)** The element num[9] is the 10th element of the array num.
- **(b)** A loop whose test condition is missing or it never evaluates to false is known as an infinite loop.
- **(c)** Infinite times.
- **(d)** The process of calling a function in such a way that the change in formal arguments reflects in actual parameters in known as call by reference.
- **(e)** The process of repeating several statements for a particular number of times is called iteration.

Question 2.
- **(a)** Give the outputs of the following codes :
  - (i)
    ```
    for (int i = 10; i > 6; i = i – 2)
    System.out.println (i);
    ```
  - (ii)
    ```
    {
    int totalcost = 6;
    int items = 12;
    System.out.println ("cost per item =" + totalcost / items);
    }
    ```
- **(b)** Evaluate the following Java expressions where a, b are integers and c, d and f are floating numbers :
  a = 1, b = 2, c = 3.0, d = 4.0, f=0·0.
  - (i)   f = a + b / a
  - (ii)   c = d * a + b
  - (iii) c = (a++) * d + a
  - (iv) f = (++b) * b – a
  - (v)   c = a – (b++) * (– d)
- **(c)** Define binary search.
- **(d)** What will "PATHSHALAA". substring (2, 5) return ?
- **(e)** Differentiate between the following :
  - (i)   While and do-while loop.
  - (ii)   Compiler and interpreter.

Answer :
- **(a)** (i)   10

           8

       (ii)   cost per item = 0
- **(b)** (i)   3.0   (ii) 6.0

       (iii) 6.0   (iv) 8.0

       (v)   9.0
- **(c)** In binary search, the system performs search operation by dividing the array elements into two halves.
- **(d)** THS

66 | *ICSE Model Specimen Papers, X*

(e) (i)

	While	Do–while
1.	It will not execute at all if the condition is not satisfied.	It execute at least once.
2.	It is an entry controlled loop.	It is an exit controlled loop.

(ii)

Compiler	Interpreter
A compiler converts all instructions to machine language at once and all errors are listed together.	An interpreter does the same but line by line.

Question 3.

Write a program to input a number and print the sum of its first and last digit.

Answer :

```
class work
{
public static void main(int n)
{
int c[ ] = new int [6];
int digit, sum = 0, i = 0;
do
{
    digit = n % 10;
    c[i] = digit;
    i++;
    n = n / 10;
}
while (n != 0);
System.out.println ("the first digit is" + c[i–1]);
System.out.println ("the last digit is" + c[0]);
System.out.println ("the sum is "+ (c[i–1] + c[0]));
}
}
```

SECTION–B

Question 4.

Write a class compute to display the following format

```
1   2   3   4   5   5   4   3   2   1
1   2   3   4           4   3   2   1
1   2   3                   3   2   1
1   2                           2   1
1                                   1
```

Answer :

(a)
```
class compute
{
public static void main()
{
int i, Q, c = 5, sp = 0;
for (int k = 1; k <= 5; k++)
{
for (i = 1; i < Q; i++)
{
System.out.print (i);
if (i == c)
{
```

```
for (f = 1, f <= sp; f++)
{
System.out.print (" ");
for (j = c; j >= 1; j--)
{
System.out.print (j);
}
c = c - 1
System.out.println ();
sp = sp + 2;
}
}
}
}
}
}
```

Question 5.

In an examination, the grades are given according to the marks obtained, WAP in Java to display the grades accordingly.

Marks	Grades
80% and above	Distinction
60% or more but less than 80%	Ist Div.
45% or more but less than 60%	IInd Div.
40% or more but less then 45%	Pass
Less than 40%	Fail

Answer :

```java
import java.io.*;
public class grades
{
public static void main(String args[]) throws IOException
{
int m;
BufferedReader in = new BufferedReader (new InputStreamReader(System.in));
System.out.println ("Enter the marks");
m = Integer.parseInt(in.readLine());
if (m >= 80)
System.out.println ("Distinction");
else if ((m >= 60) && (m < 80))
System.out.println ("First Division");
else if ((m >= 45) && (m < 60))
System.out.println ("Second Division")
else if ((m >= 40) && (m < 45))
System.out.println ("Pass");
else
System.out.println ("Fail");
}
}
```

Question 6.

WAP in Java to print all perfect numbers between 1 to 100.

A perfect number is one which is equal to the sum of its factors. e.g. $6 = 1 + 2 + 3$

Answer :

```java
class series
{
public static void main()
{
int sum;
for (int i = 1; i <= 100; i++)
{
    sum = 0;
    for (int j = 1; j <= i – 1; j++)
    {
       if (i % j == 0)
       sum = sum +j;
    }
    if (sum == i)
    System.out.println (i + "is a perfect number");
}
}
}
```

Question 7.

WAP to input a number and search it in the given list using binary search technique.
list = 3, 10, 17, 25, 56, 79

Answer :

```java
class searching
{
    int A[ ] = {3, 10, 17, 25, 56, 79};
    int l, h, mid, flag = 0;
    void display(int n)
    {
    l = 0;
    h = A.length – 1;
    while (l <= h)
    {
        mid = (l + h)/2;
        if (n > A[mid])
            l = mid + 1;
        else if (n < A[mid])
            h = mid – 1;
        else
        {
            flag = 1;
            break;
        }
    }
    if (flag == 1)
    {
        System.out.println ("Number found at index" + mid);
    }
    else
    {
        System.out.println ("Number not found");
    }
    }
}
```

Question 8.

WAP to calculate the sum of the series :

$S = a/1 + a/2 + a/3 + \dots\dots\dots\dots\dots a/n$

where

$a = 2$

$n = 10$

Answer :

```
class work
{
public static void main(String args[ ])
{
int x, a = 2, n = 10;
double sum = 0.0;
for (x = 1; x <= n; x++)
{
sum = sum + (float) (a/x);
}
System.out.println ("The sum of the series is" + sum);
}
}
```

Question 9.

WAP to input eight numbers and arrange them in ascending order using bubble sort.

Answer :

```
import java.util.*;
class sort
{
    int A[ ] = new int [8];
    int i, j, t;
    void display( )
    {
        Scanner sc = new Scanner(System.in);
        for (i = 0; i < 8; i++)
        {
        System.out.println ("Enter a number");
        A[i]=sc.nextInt( );
        }
        for (i = 0; i < 8; i++)
        {
            for (j = 0; j < 7 - i; j++)
            {
                if (A[j] > A[j + 1])
                {
                        t   =  A[j];
                    A[j]  =  A[j + 1];
                  A[j+1]  =  t;
                }
            }
        }
        for (i = 0; i < 8; i++)
        {
            System.out.println (A[i]);
        }
    }
}
```

MODEL SPECIMEN PAPER–15

SECTION—A

Question 1.

(a) What is an object ? Give example of some real world objects.

(b) What are literals ? Explain with an example.

(c) Name two fractional numeric data types used in Java.

(d) Differentiate between encapsulation and abstraction.

(e) Define function.

Question 2.

(a) Differentiate between the following with the help of an examples :

    (i) If and if–else statement.

    (ii) Break and continue statement.

    (iii) While and do-while statement.

    (iv) Char and String data type.

(b) What is call by reference ?

(c) Perform the following :

Define the following data members with the respective data types

    (i) Temperature

    (ii) Age

    (iii) Name

(d) What will be the output of the following code :

```
char chars[] = {'A', 'B', 'C'};
String S1 = new string (chars);
String S2 = new string (S1);
System.out.println (S1);
System.out.println (S2);
```

Question 3.

(a) What will be the output of the following code :

```
char ch = 'A';
int n;
n = ch = = 'a' ? 'a' : 'A';
System.out.println (n);
```

SECTION-B

Question 4.

WAP to calculate the sum of the following series using nested for loop

$$S = (1) + (1 + 2) + (1 + 2 + 3) + (1 + 2 + 3 + 4) + \ldots\ldots\ldots N$$

where N is input.

Question 5.

Suppose there are three arrays X, Y, Z with m, n and m + n number of elements respectively. Arrange the elements of Y in descending order using bubble sort method.

Question 6.

WAP in Java to accept a number and check :

(a) Whether the no. is divisible by 2 and 5.

(b) Whether the no. is divisible by 2 but not by 5.

(c) Whether the no. is divisible by 5 but not by 2.

The program must display the message accordingly.

Question 7.

WAP in Java to accept a number and display its reverse.

Question 8.

WAP in Java to accept a word and display it in the following format

e.g. : Input   : Hello

      Output : Hello

                  Hell

                  Hel

                  He

                  H

Question 9.

Define a class with a function to count the number of words in a string where each word is separated by a blank space and the string terminates by a period.

MODEL SPECIMEN PAPER–16

SECTION—A

Question 1.
- **(a)** Define loops.
- **(b)** Can Modulus operator be applied to all kinds of datatypes ?
- **(c)** Can a variable name start with a zero ?
- **(d)** Are both these statements same ?

```
a+=b;
a=a+b;
```

- **(e)** Values are assigned to a variable using which operator ?

Answer :
- **(a)** Loops are segments of code that are repeated either for a designated number of times or until a certain test statement or expression is true.
- **(b)** No, modulus operator cannot be applied to all kinds of data types.
- **(c)** No, a variable name cannot start with a zero.
- **(d)** Yes, both the statements, a + = b; and a = a + b; are the same.
- **(e)** Assignment operator is used to assign values to a variable.

Question 2.
- **(a)** Give the output

```java
{
    double x=15.5, b=4.3;
    System.out.println ("x="+x);
    System.out.println ("y="+y);
    System.out.println ("x+y=" +(x+y));
    System.out.println (" x–y= " +(x–y));
    System.out.println ("x*y=" +(x*y));
    System.out.println ("x / y="+(x / y));
    System.out.println ("x%y="+(x%y));
}
```

- **(b)** Give the output

```java
class even10
{
public static void main()
{
int ctr;
for (ctr = 1; ctr <= 10; ctr++)
{
    System.out.print (ctr+" ");
    if (ctr%2 == 0)
        continue;
    System.out.println ("  ");
}
}
}
```

- **(c)** Give the syntax of do–while loop.
- **(d)** WAP to find the factorial of a number using while loop only.
- **(e)** Is continue statement used in switch statement ?

Answer :
(a) x = 15.5
     y = 4.3
     x+y = 19.8
     x–y = 11.2
     x*y = 195.65
     x/y = 3.60465
     x%y = 2.6

(b) 1
     2   3
     4   5
     6   7
     8   9
     10

(c) do
     {
         body of statements;
     }
     while (condition);

(d) class loop
     {
     public static void main(int n)
     {
     int a;
     double fact;
     a=1;
     fact= 1;
     while (a <= n)
     {
         fact = fact*a;
         a++;
     }
     System.out.println (" Factorial of "+n+" is "+fact);
     }
     }

(e) No, continue statement cannot be used in switch statement.

Question 3.
(a) Define class.
(b) Name the levels of visibility of data members of a class.
(c) Define a string.

Answer :
(a) A class is a collection of objects. It is a user defined aggregate datatype.
(b) The three levels of visibility are
     (i) public   (ii) private   (iii) protected
(c) String is a series of characters
     e.g. : "HELLO".

SECTION—B

Question 4.
In an election, two candidates A and B contested in which A got 60% of the votes. WAP to calculate the number of votes each candidate got taking total no. of votes as input.

Answer :
public class election
{
public static void main(int votes)
{
    double V1, V2;

```
V1=(double) (60/100*votes);
V2=votes–V1;
System.out.println ("The total no. of notes=" +votes);
System.out.println ("No. of votes first candidate got=" + (int) V1);
System.out.println ("No. of votes second candidate got=" +(int)V2);
   }
}
```

Question 5.

The standard form of quadratic equation is given by $ax^2 + bx + c = 0$, where $d = b^2 - 4*a*c$, is known as discrimant which determines the nature of roots of the equation accordingly.

  if d>=0; Roots are real and unequal

  if d=0; Roots are real and equal

  if d<0; Roots are imaginary

Answer :

```
import java.io.*;
public class roots
{
public static void main (String args[ ]) throws IOException
{
   int a, b, c;
   double d;
   BufferedReader in = new BufferedReader (new InputStreamReader(System.in));
   System.out.println ("Enter value of a, b, c");
   a=Integer.parseInt(in.readLine());
   b=Integer.parseInt(in.readLine());
   c=Integer.parseInt(in.readLine());
   d=Math.sqrt(b*b – 4*a*c);
   if (d > 0)
      System.out.println ("Roots are real and unequal");
   if (d = = 0)
      System.out.println ("Roots are real and equal");
   if (d < 0)
      System.out.println ("Roots are imaginary");
   }
}
```

Question 6.

Wap in Java to display the first 10 numbers of the fibonacci series.

Answer :

```
public class Fibonacci
{
public static void main( )
{
   int a, b, c;
   a = 0; b=1;
   c = 0;
   n = 3;
   System.out.println ("The series is");
   System.out.println (a);
   System.out.println (b);
   do
```

```
        {
            c = a+b;
            System.out.println (c);
            a = b;
            b = c;
            n = n+1;
        }
        while (n <= 10);
    }
}
```

Question 7.

WAP in Java to accept a word and display the same in Piglatin form. A word is said to be Piglatin by framing a new word with the first vowel present in the word with the remaining words present before the first vowel and ended with 'ay'.

Answer :

```
import java.io.*;
class piglatin
{
public static void main(String args[ ]) throws IOException
{
BufferedReader in = new BufferedReader (new InputStreamReader(System.in));
int x, y;
String a, c, d;
char b;
b = 0;
System.out.println ("Enter the string");
a = in.readLine( );
x = a.length( );
System.out.println ("The piglatin form is");
for (y = 0; y < x; y++)
{
b = a.charAt(y);
if(b == 'a') | | (b == 'e') | | (b == 'i') | | (b == 'o') | | (b == 'u') | | (b == 'A') | | (b == 'E') | | (b == 'I') | | (b == 'o')
| | (b == 'u'))
break;
}
c = a.substring(y, x);
d = a.substring(0, y);
System.out.println (c+d+"ay");
}
}
```

Question 8.

WAP in Java to display the following pattern using arrays

```
1
1 1
1 2 1
1 3 3 1
1 4 6 4 1
```

Answer :

```
import java.io.*;
public class pascal
{
public static void main(String args[ ]) throws IOException
{
```

```
BufferedReader in = new BufferedReader (new InputStreamReader(System.in));
int i, j, n;
int m[ ]=new int [20];
System.out.println ("Enter size");
n=Integer.parseInt(in.readLine( ));
m[0] = 1;
for (i = 0; i < n; i++)
{
    for (r = 0; j <= i; j++)
    {
        System.out.print (m[j] +" ");
        System.out.println ( );
        for (j = i + 1; j >= 1; j--)
        {
            m[j] = m[j] + m[j – 1]
        }
    }
}
}
}
```

Question 9.

WAP to input a number and check whether it is Armstrong number or not.

Answer :

```
import java.util.*;
class Arm
{
        int n, t, d, s = 0;
        void display( )
            {
                Scanner sc = new Scanner(System.in);
                System.out.println ("Enter a number");
                n = sc.nextInt( );
                t = n;
                while (n > 0)
                {
                    d = n%10;
                    s = s + d*d*d;
                    n = n /10;
                }
                if (S == t)
                {
                    System.out.println ("Armstrong Number");
                }
                    else
                {
                    System.out.println ("Not Armstrong number ");
                }
            }
    }
```

MODEL SPECIMEN PAPER–17

SECTION—A

Question 1.

(a) A single dimensional array contains N elements. What will be the last subscript ?

(b) What will be the result of evaluating the following expression :

$$1/2 + 3.5 * 2.0$$

(c) Give an equivalent Java expression for the following equation :

$$1/3\,ab + 1/2\,cd$$

(d) Why is default case used in switch case statement ?

(e) What is the role of try and catch keyword in exception handling ?

Answer :

(a) N-1

(b) 7.0

(c) 1/3*a*b+1/2*c*d

(d) When none of the case matches, the control goes to default case.

(e) Try contains a block of statements to perform. Any error occurring within the try block is trapped. Further a report is to be passed to the exception handler about the error, which is caught by the catch block.

Question 2.

(a) Give the output :

(i)
```
int a[ ] = {2, 4, 6, 8};
for (i = 0; i <= 1; i++)
{
    s = a[i] + a[3 – i];
    System.out.println (s);
}
```

(ii)
```
{
    int value = 0;
    int count = 1;
    value = ++count;
    System.out.println ("Value :" + value +" ; " + " count :" + count);
}
```

(b) Differentiate between

(i) selection control statements and iteration control statements.

(ii) print ( ) and println ( )

(c) Consider the following statement

$$string\ X = "14";$$

Convert the string data X to double type.

(d) Suppose a = "Computer". What will a.indexof('m'); return ?

(e) Write the function of trim( ) with an example.

Answer :

(a) (i) 10

10

(ii) Value : 2; count : 2

(b) (i)

Selection Control Statements	Iteration Control Statements
Selection control statements refer to transfer of control depending upon the given condition and a selection is made depending on the given options.	Iteration statements act as automatic looping statements. Here, the compound statements are executed again and again until a given condition is met.

(ii)	**print ()**	**println ()**
	It prints the data on the screen.	It prints the data on the screen as well as, directs the control on the next line.

(c) double d = Double.parseDouble (x);

(d) 2

(e) Trim removes all white spaces of the beginning and at the end of the string

e.g. a ="................. Rajendra Vidyalaya";

a = a.trim();

output : Rajendra Vidyalaya

Question 3.

(a) Consider the following statements

```
class equal
{
    public static void main(String args[ ] )
    String S1 = "Hello";
    String S2 = "good morning";
    System.out.println (S1 + "equals" + S2 + "→" + S1.equals(S2));
    System.out.println (S1 + "→" + S2 + "→" + (S1 == S2));
}
```

(b) What does the following statements mean ?

employee staff = new employee ();

(c) Consider the following quadratic equation

$$Y = ax^2 + bx + c$$

Write a program to solve the equation

(i) if x > = 4 && y = – ax² + bx – c;

(ii) If x < 4

Answer :

(a) Hello equals good morning false

Hello → goodmorning → false

(b) new operator allocates memory and call constructor employee( ).

(c)
```
import java.io;
class text
{
    public static void main() throws IOException
    {
        int a, b, c, x, y;
        BufferedReader input = new BufferedReader (new InputStreamReader(System.in));
        System.out.println ("Enter the value of x");
        String VI = input.readLine();
        x = Integer.parseInt(VI);
        System.out.print ("Enter the value of b =");
        String V3 input.readLine( )
        b = Integer.parseInt(V3),
        System.out.print ("Enter Values of C");
        String V4 = input.readLine();
        c = Integer.parseInt(V4);
        if (x >= 4)
        System.out.println ("value of y = "+ (a * x * x + b * x + c));
        else
        System.out.println ("value of y =" + (– a * x * x + b * x – c));
    }
}
```

SECTION—B

Question 4.

Write a class with name employee and basic as its data members, to find the gross pay of an employee of the following allowances and deductions.

$$DA = 25\% \text{ of basic pay}$$
$$HRA = 15\% \text{ ''} \qquad \text{''}$$
$$PF = 8.33\% \text{ ''} \qquad \text{''}$$
$$\text{Net Pay} = \text{Basic pay} + DA + HRA$$
$$\text{Gross Pay} = \text{Net Pay} - PF$$

Answer :

```java
import java.io.*;
public class employee
{
public static void main(String args[ ]) throws IOException
{
int basic;
double hra, da, pf, npay, gross;
gross = 0;
BufferedReader in = new BufferedReader (new InputStreamReader(System.in));
System.out.println ("Enter basic salary");
basic = Integer.parseInt(in.readLine());
da = basic * 25 / 100;
bra = basic * 15 / 100;
pf = basic * 8.33 / 100;
npay = da + hra + basic;
gross = npay - pf;
System.out.println ("The net pay =" + npay);
System.out.println ("The gross pay =" + gross);
}
}
```

Question 5.

WAP using a function called area() to compute the area of a :

(i)   Circle (πr^2) where $\pi = 3.14$

(ii) Square (side * side)

(iii) Rectangle (length * breadth)

Display the menu to output the area as per user's choice.

Answer :

```java
import java.io.*;
public class list
{
public static void circlearea(double r)
{
double a = 3.14*r*r;
System.out.println ("Area of circle" + a);
}
public static void squarearea(double side)
{
double a = side * side;
System.out.println ("Area of square =" + a);
}
```

```java
public static void rectanglearea(double length, double breadth)
{
double a = length * breadth;
System.out.println ("Area of rectangle =" + a);
}
public static void main() throws IOException
{
String S;
int ch;
BufferedReader br = new BufferedReader (new InputStreamReader(System in));
System.out.pintln ("Main");
System.out.println ("1. Circle Area");
System.out.println ("2. Square Area");
System.out.println ("3. Rectangle Area");
S = br.readLine( );
ch = Integer.parseInt(S);
switch (ch)
{
case 1 :
        System.out.println ("Enter radius");
        double r = Double.parseDouble(br.readLine());
        circle area(r);
        break;
case 2 :
        System.out.println ("Enter Side");
        double side = Double.parseDouble(br.readLine());
        squarearea(side);
        break;
case 3 :
        System.out.println ("Enter length");
        double l = Double.parseDouble(br.readLine());
        System.out.println ("Enter breadth");
        double b = Double.parseDouble(br.readLine());
        rectanglearea(l, b);
        break;
default :
        System.out.println ("Invalid Choice");
}
}
}
```

Question 6.

Write a class to display a word in the following pattern

sample Input :   BLUEJ

e.g. : Output :   B

                   L

                   U

                   E

                   J

Answer :

```
import java.io.*;
public class pattern
{
public static void main(String args[]) throws IOException
{
BufferedReader in = new BufferedReader (new InputStreamReader(System in));
String name;
int a, y;
System.out.println ("Enter your word");
name = in.readLine();
y = name.length();
for (a = 0; a < y; a++)
System.out.println (name.charAt(a));
}
}
```

Question 7.

Write a program to input the accident records of 75 drivers and print the number of drivers below 20 yrs. of age, those between 20 and 30 yrs. of age and those above 30 yrs. of age. Also print the % of female drivers who have met with an accident.

Answer :

```
import java.io.*;
class rest
{
public static void main() throws IOException
{
BufferedReader br = new BufferedReader (new InputStreamReader(System.in));
int ag, c, d, e, f;
String sx, nm;
c = d = e = f = 0;
double pf = 0;
for (int i = 1; <= 75; i++)
{
    System.out.println ("Enter name");
    nm = br.readLine();
    System.out.println ("Enter Sex");
    sx = br.readLine();
    System.out.println ("Enter age");
    ag = Integer.parseInt(br.readLine());
    if (ag < 20)
    c = c + 1;
    else if (ag >= 20 && ag <= 30)
    d = d + 1;
    else if (ag > 30)
    e = e + 1;
```

```
        if (sx.equals(Female))
        f++;
}
pf = f*100/75.0;
System.out.println ("Drivers below 20" +c);
System.out.println ("Drivers 20-30 yrs." +d);
System.out.println ("Drivers > 30 yrs." +e);
System.out.println ("Percentage of female drives who met with an accident" +pf);
}
}
```

Question 8.

WAP to enter a number and sort the digit in ascending order. Display the new digit obtained.

Answer :

```
class work
{
public static void main(int n)
{
int a[ ] = new int [10];
int b, d, s = 0;
while (n > 0)
{
d = n % 10;
a[s] = d;
s = s + 1;
n = n / 10;
}
for (int i = 0; i < s – 1; i++)
{
for (int j = i + 1; j < s; j++)
{
if (a[i] > a[j])
{
j = a[i];
a = a[j];
a[j] =j;
}
}
}
for (int g = 0; g < s; g++)
{
System.out.print (a[g]);
}
}
}
```

Question 9.

WAP to input a number and check whether it is an automorphic number or not.

Answer :

```
class check
{
    int t, c=0, sq, p;
    void display(int n)
    {
        t = n;
        sq = n*n;
        while (t > 0)
        {
            c++;
            t = t/10;
        }
        P = (int) Math.pow(10, c);
        if (sq % P = = n)
        {
            System.out.println ("Automorphic Number");
        }
        else
        {
            System.out.println ("Not an Automorphic Number");
        }
    }
}
```

MODEL SPECIMEN PAPER–18

SECTION—A

Question 1.

(a) Write the difference between :
  (i) do while and while Loop.
  (ii) Implicit type casting and explicit type casting.
  (iii) if-else and switch.

(b) Explain the increment-decrement operators with an example program.

Question 2.

(a) Fill in the blanks :
  (i) ? : operator is also called as ....
  (ii) Maximum storage of data type double is ....
  (iii) \t character is used to give ....
  (iv) .... prints the statement on the same line.
  (v) Java is of dual utility..................... and ....

(b) Read the following program and answer the given questions :

```
class demo
{
    public void main()
    {
        char str[ ] = {`c', `o', `m', `p', `u', `t', `e', `r' };
        String a=new String (str);
        System.out.println (a.length());
    }
}
```

  (i) What will be the length of array str ?
  (ii) What will be the output of the above program ?

Question 3.

(a) Write the output of following code :

```
class output
{
    public void fmn( )
    {
        int a=12, b=10;
        System.out.println ("a++="+ a++);
        System.out.println ("a>b="+ (a>b));
        System.out.println ("++a=" + ++ a);
        System.out.println ("--a="+ --a);
        System.out.println ("a!=(a+b)="+ (a!=(a+b)));
    }
}
```

(b) Find the errors if any in the following program :

```
Class 12design
{
    public void mn
    {
        byte a=10;
        int b=20;
```

```
            int c=a>b?a, b;
            System.out.println ('The value of c is :"+c);
    }
}
```

SECTION—B

Question 4.

    (a) Using Switch case create class which takes the day number (1-7) as input and prints the corresponding day in words. *e.g.* : 3-WEDNESDAY 5-FRIDAY.

    (b) Write a class to input a number and print its odd factors.

Question 5.

    (a) Create a class to print the following pattern :

```
1
12
123
1234
12345
```

    (b) Create a class to print the following pattern :

```
+++++
++++
+++
++
+
```

Question 6.

Write a class to enter a number and check whether it is palindrome or not.

Question 7.

    (a) Write a class fact which takes an integer number as input and then prints its factorial value.

        e.g. : Factorial of 5=1*2*3*4*5 (use do–while loop)

    (b) Create a class to take an integer number as input and print all its factors.

        e.g. : Factors of 6 are 1,2,3,6 (use for loop).

Question 8.

    (a) Write a class to print the following series $S=a/1+a/2+a/3+a/4\ldots\ldots\ldots a/n$.

    (b) Write a class fibo10 to display the first 10 terms of Fibonacci series.

Question 9.

Create a class to print the following series : (Where a and n are user inputs)

$-1/a+2/a-3/a+4/a\ldots\ldots\ldots\ldots n/a$.

●●

MODEL SPECIMEN PAPER–19

SECTION—A

Question 1.
- **(a)** How is a package declared ?
- **(b)** Define an identifier.
- **(c)** Why is data hiding implemented ?
- **(d)** Define single inheritance.
- **(e)** What is the function of toLowerCase( ) ?

Answer :
- **(a)** A package is declared by using the keyword package followed by the package name.
- **(b)** The name of an item in a program is known as identifier.
- **(c)** Data hiding is implemented to insulate data from direct access by the outside world.
- **(d)** When a derived class derives properties from one base class, it is called single inheritance.
- **(e)** toLowerCase() is used to convert a string to lower case.

Question 2.
- **(a)** Give outputs
  - (i)

```
class even
{
public static void main()
{
    StringBuffer str=new StringBuffer ("COMPUTER SCIENCE");
    System.out.println ("Original String = " +str);
    str.reverse();
    System.out.println ("Reversed string = " +str);
}
}
```

- **(b)** What happens when the code gets evaluated ?

```
{
    double a, b;
    a=Math.pow(b,3);
}
```

- **(c)** Write a statement to convert a string "evergreen" into upper case.
- **(d)** Give the general syntax of declaration of an array.
- **(e)** Define linear search.

Answer:
- **(a)** Original string = COMPUTER SCIENCE
  Reversed String = ECNEICS RETUPMOC
- **(b)** The cube of b gets assigned to a.
- **(c)** evergreen.toUpperCase( );
- **(d)** datatype arrayname[ ] = newdatatype [size]; e.g. : int A[ ] = new int [25].
- **(e)** Linear search is a technique in which the searching of an item begins at the start of an array. The process continues one after another, where each element of array is checked and compared with a given data item till the end of the array location is reached.

Question 3.
- **(a)** The following number (89, 20, 31, 56, 20, 64, 48) are required to be sorted using selection sort.

  Show how the list would appear after each pass.
- **(b)** What is a variable and a constant ?
- **(c)** Write the function of replace().
- **(d)** What will be the result of the following two expressions if i=10 initially ?
  - (i) ++i <= 10
  - (ii) i++ <= 10

Answer :

(a) Ist pass   : 20, 89, 31, 56, 20, 64, 48
     IInd pass : 20, 20, 31, 56, 89, 64, 48
     IIIrd pass : 20, 20, 31, 56, 89, 64, 48
     IVth pass : 20, 20, 31, 56, 89, 64, 56
     Vth pass : 20, 20, 31, 48, 56, 64, 89
     VIth pass : 20, 20, 31, 48, 56, 64, 89
     VIIth pass : 20, 20, 31, 48, 56, 64, 89

(b) Variable : It is defined as a location in the memory of the computer where the values are stored and can be changed. A constant is the value which cannot be changed.

(c) It replaces all the occurrences of the *e.g.,* string.during the executed of the program.

Syntax : a.replace ('m', 'n'); *e.g.,* string.during the executed of the program.

(d) (i)   false   (ii) true

SECTION–B

Question 4.

WAP to display the sum and the average of all even and odd numbers between 1 and 100.

Answer :

```
class test1
{
public static void main( )
{
int, a, b, c, d, sum1=0, sum2=0; double avg1, avg2;
for (a = 1; a <= 100; a++)
{
if (a%2 == 0)
    sum1 = sum1+a;
else
    sum2 = sum2+a;
}
avg1=sum1/50;
avg2=sum2/50;
System.out.println ("The sum of even no.s is" +sum1);
System.out.println ("and the average is" +avg1);
System.out.println ("The sum of odd numbers is" + sum2);
System.out.println ("and the average is" + avg2);
}
}
```

Question 5.

WAP to calculate the sum of the following series.

$$S = 1/2 - 2/3 + 3/4 \ldots\ldots\ldots\ldots 10/11$$

Answer :

```
public class special
{
public static void main( )
{
double a, s;
s=0;
for (a=1; a <= 10; a++)
{
if (a%2 == 0)
s=s–a/(a + 1);
else
s=s+a/(a + 1);
```

```
}
System.out.println ("The sum of series is=" +s);
}
}
```

Question 6.

WAP to input a given string to calculate the total number of characters and vowels present in the string and also reverse the string.

Example
Input
Enter String : SNOWY
Output

Total Number of Characters	:	5
No. of vowels	:	1
Reverse String	:	YWONS

Answer :

```
import java.io.*;
public class test
{
public static void main(String args[ ]) throws IOException
{
String s, rev="";
char ch;
int vowel=0;
BufferedReader br = new BufferedReader (new InputStreamReader(System.in));
System.out.println ("Enter String");
s=br.readLine();
s=s.toLowerCase();
int l=s.length();
for (int i = 0; i < l; i++)
{
ch=s.charAt(i);
if (ch == 'a' || ch == 'e' || ch == 'i' || ch == 'o' || ch == 'u')
{
vowels++;
}
}
for (int i=(l – 1); i >= 0; i––)
{
ch=s.charAt(i);
rev=rev+ch;
}
System.out.println ("Total No. of characters" + l);
System.out.println ("Total no. of vowels" + vowel);
System.out.println ("Reversed String is" + rev);
}
}
```

Question 7.

WAP in Java to make a simple calculator, which can perform mainly the function of addition, subtraction, multiplication and division. Input should be accepted from the keyboard.

Answer :

```
import java.io.*;
import java.lang.*;
class calculator
{
```

```java
public static void main(String args[ ]) throws IOException
{
double a, b, result;
result= 0;
int choice;
BufferedReader input = new BufferedReader (new InputStreamReader(System.in));
System.out.println ("Enter first no");
String V1 =input.readLine( );
a=Double.parseDouble(V1);
System.out.println ("Enter 2nd no.");
String V2=input.readLine( );
b=Double.parseDouble(V2);
System.out.println ("Enter 1 for addition");
System.out.println ("Enter 2 for subtraction");
System.out.println ("Enter 3 for multiplication");
System.out.println ("Enter 4 for division");
String n=input.readLine( );
choice = Integer.parseInt(n);
if (choice == 1)
{
    result=a+b;
    System.out.println ("Result=" + result);
}
else if (choice == 2)
{
    result=a–b;
    System.out.println ("Result=" + result);
}
else if (choice == 3)
{
    result=a*b;
    System.out.println ("Result=" + result)
}
else if (choice == 4)
{
    result=a/b;
    System.out.println ("Result=" + result);
}
else
    System.out.println ("Wrong Choice");
}
}
```

Question 8.

WAP in Java to print the following format :

```
1
2    3    2
3    4    5    4    3
4    5    6    7    6    5    4
5    6    7    8    7    6    5    4    3
```

Answer :

```
class Pattern
{
public static void main( )
{
int a, b, c,;
for (a = 1; a <= 5; a++)
{
for (c = 1; c <= a; c++)
{
System.out.println (b);
}
}
b=b-2;
for (c = 1; c < b; c++)
{
System.out.println (b);
}
}
}
```

Question 9.

WAP to input a number and check whether it is a special number or not.

Answer :

```
import java.util.*;
class Special
{
    int n, t, d, f, i, s = 0;
    void display( );
    {
        Scanner sc = newScanner(System.in);
        System.out.println ("Enter a no.");
        n = sc.nextInt( );
        t = n;
        while (n > 0)
        {
            d = n % 10;
            f = 1;
            for (i = 1; i <= d; i++)
            {
                f = f*i;
            }
            s = s + f;
            n = n / 10;
        }
        if (s = = t)
                System.out.println ("Special No.");
        else
                System.out.println ("Not a special No.");
    }
}
```

MODEL SPECIMEN PAPER–20

SECTION—A

Question 1.
- **(a)** Name the types of constructor in Java.
- **(b)** Explain a class in a Java program.
- **(c)** What are pure and impure functions.
- **(d)** Explain the formal and actual parameters in a method.
- **(e)** Define polymorphism.

Answer:
- **(a)** The different types of constructors are :
  - (i) Non–parameterised constructor
  - (ii) Parameterised constructor
  - (iii) Default constructor
- **(b)** A class represents a set of objects that share some common characteristics and behaviour. It is an object maker or producer.
- **(c)** Pure function returns some value from function to the caller about the state of an object. It allows access to the state of an abject.

  Impure function may or may not return a value. It basically change the state of an object each time it is called.
- **(d)** The parameters which receive the value during function call from the caller are known as formal parameters.

  The values which are passed to the method during its call from the caller are known as actual parameters.
- **(e)** Polymorphism is a process to create a method with the same name but different parameters that matches up the method's name and executes the relevant method.

Question 2.

Write short notes on following :
- **(a)** Constructors
- **(b)** Difference between "call by value" and "call by reference method".
- **(c)** "this" keyword
- **(d)** Inheritance.

Answer :
- **(a)** A constructor is a member function of the class with a name same as that of the class name used to initialize the instant variables of the objects.
- **(b)** Call by value is process of passing a copy of actual arguments to the formal parameters. Any change made in the formal parameters does not reflect the actual arguments.

  Call by references is the process of passing the address of actual arguments to the formal parameters and any change will be reflected in the actual arguments.
- **(c)** Sometimes, in a member method "this" keyword is needed to use the object in which the method is called. It is also used to differentiate between local and global variables when they both have the same name.
- **(d)** Inheritance means to acquire some properties of one class and pass them to the other class.

Question 3.

Name one symbol for following :
- **(a)** Relational operator
- **(b)** Logical operator
- **(c)** Bitwise operator
- **(d)** Arithmetic operator
- **(e)** Unary operator

Answer :

(a) == (Assignment Operator).

(b) && (And Operator).

(c) << (Shift left Bitwise Operator).

(d) % (Modulus Operator).

(e) ++ (Increment Operator).

SECTION—B

Question 4.

Write a program to enter a sentence from the keyboard and count the number of times a particular word occurs in it. Display the frequency of the search word.

Example :

INPUT

Enter a sentence : the quick brown fox jumps over the lazy dog.

Enter a word to be searched : the

OUTPUT :

Searched word occurs : 2 times.

Answer :

```
import java.io.*;
class test
{
public static void main( ) throws IOException
{
char c; int ent = 0;
BufferedReader br = new BufferedReader (new InputStreamReader(System.in));
System.out.println ("Enter a sentence");
Strings = br.readLine( ):
System.out.println ("enter a word to be searched");
StringW=br.readLine( );
String n = " ";
for (int i = 0; i < s.length( ); i++)
{
    c = s.charAt(i);
    if (n.equals (w))
    {
        ent = ent + 1;
        n = " ";
    }
    else
    {
        n = n + c;
    }
}
System.out.println ("frequency of word is "+ ent);
}
}
```

Question 5.

WAP in Java to print the following pattern

```
a
a a
a a a
a a a a
a a a a a
```

Answer :

```java
class pattern
{
public static void main( )
{
int i, j;
for (i = 1; i <= 5; i++)
{
for (j = 1; j <= i; j++)
System.out.print ("a");
System.out.println ( );
}
}
}
```

Question 6.

WAP to display the sum of the following series

$$S = 1/2 - 2/3 - 3/4 \ldots\ldots\ldots\ldots 10/11.$$

Answer :

```java
class spl
{
public static void main( )
{
double a, s;
s=0;
for (a = 1; a <= 10; a++)
{
s = s - a/(a+1);
}
System.out.println ("The sum is" +s);
}
}
```

Question 7.

WAP in Java to accept the number of days and displays, it after converting them into no. of years, months and days.

Answer :

```java
import java.io.*;
class days
{
public static void main() throws IOException
{
int a, b, c, y, d;
BufferedReader in = new BufferedReader (new InputStreamReader(System.in));
System.out.println ("Enter the no. of days");
a=Integer.parseInt(in.readLine( ));
y=a/365;
b=a%365;
c=b/30;
```

```
d=b%30;
System.out.println ("Years="+y);
System.out. println ("Months="+c);
System.out.println ("Days="+d);
}
}
```

Question 8.

WAP in Java to accept a number and find all its factors.

Answer :

```
import java.io.*;
class factors
{
public static void main(int n)
{
int a;
for (a = 1; a <= n; a++)
{
if (n%a == 0)
System.out.println (a+"is a factor of"+n);
}
}
}
```

Question 9.

WAP to generate the following pascal's triangle.

```
1
1  1
1  2  1
1  3  3  1
1  4  6  4  1
```

Answer :

```
import java.io.*;
class pascal
{
public static void main() throws IOException
{
BufferedReader in = new BufferedReader (new InputStreamReader(System.in));
int i, j, n;
int m[ ]=new int [20];
System.out.println ("Enter the size of the pascal triangle");
n=Integer.parseInt(in.readLine( ));
m[0]=1;
for (i = 0; k < n; i++)
{
for (j = 0; j <= i; j++)
System.out.print (m[j]+" ");
System.out.println ( );
for (j = i+1; j > 0; j—)
m[j] = m[j] + m[j – 1];
}
}
}
```

MODEL SPECIMEN PAPER–21

SECTION—A

Question 1.
  (a) Mention any two return types of a method.
  (b) What are the smallest and largest integer values for the datatype short ?
  (c) Name the primitive datatype to represent real numbers.
  (d) Write the equivalent while loop for the following loop for(;;) {(s;)/*} where s is a statement.
  (e) What will be the value of $((1/0.0) - (1/-0.0))$.

Question 2.
  (a) Differentiate between the following :
      (i)   equals() and equalsIgnoreCase()
      (ii)   charAt() and length()
      (iii) startsWith() and endsWith().
  (b) How many bytes are used to represent the datatype int ?
  (c) Modulus operator is used under what circumstances ?
  (d) What is meant by initialization ?
  (e) State what how the values of a and b keeps on changing in the code given below :

```
{
    int a = 34;
    int b = 29;
    System.out.println ("a is" + (a++));
    System.out.println ("b is" + (b++));
    System.out.println ("Now a is" +a);
    System.out.println ("Now b is" +b);
    System.out.println ("Now a is" + (++a));
    System.out.println ("Now b is" + (++b));
}
```

Question 3.
  (a) Mention any two elements required for class declaration.
  (b) Define for loop with its syntax.

SECTION—B

Question 4.
  Write a program to display the following names in ascending order using bubble sort technique

  Yogita

  Dheeraj

  Shruti

  Shashank

Question 5.
  Write a class using string functions to accept a word and print the same in alphabetical order.

Question 6.

A wholeseller offers discount to his retailers according to the following tariff.

Goods Worth	Discount
Upto R 5,000	5%
> R 5000 and upto R 10,000/-	10%
> R 10,000 and upto R 20,000/-	15%
> R 20,000	20%

WAP to accept the total sales and calculate the discount for the goods purchased.

Question 7.

Define a class series to calculate the sum of the following series :

S = (1*2) + (2*3) + ………….. + (19*20)

Question 8.

WAP to input any 10 numbers. Calculate and print the minimum and the maximum numbers.

Question 9.

WAP to compute the sum of the first and the last digit of a number entered by the user.

●●

9 789387 660342